EIGHT - FANTASTICAL TALES FROM HERE, THERE & EVERYWHERE

POORNIMA MANCO

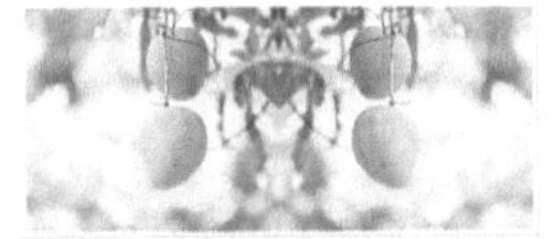

For everyone who believed in me... Thank you!

≈

"I am a great admirer of mystery and magic. Look at this life - all mystery and magic."
— Harry Houdini

≈

CONTENTS

FOREWORD

These stories contain many foreign words/terms, the explanations of which can be found in the glossary at the end of the book. This is purely for the purposes of clarity. However, if it mars the flow of the narrative for you, you can go ahead and read the book without flipping backwards and forwards. The context should make the meaning abundantly clear.

Happy reading!

THE INVISIBLE SUITCASE

" *Alors*[1]! This is it, Minou. The exact spot I've been looking for. Oh, you need not turn up your nose that way, you have yet to see what I will do to it."

The woman and the cat looked at each other; the woman looked away first. They were, at first glance, an odd couple. She was large and messy, with several bracelets jangling on her wrists, her red hair pinned in a careless up-do, curls escaping down her back, and the mauves and pinks of her outfit clashing terribly with the red lipstick she'd put on in a slapdash manner. Her bag had seen better days; nearly all the tiny mirrors having fallen away, the glint of the gold embroidery long tarnished, the straps frayed to almost nothing. A battered suitcase sat by her side, filled with the memorabilia of a long and adventurous life. Long chains hung from her neck, nestling comfortably on her large bosom. The handkerchief hem of her skirt trailed on the floor, picking up the dirt and dust of her journey. In fact, the brown leather sandals on her feet were the only sensible item on her person.

The cat, on the other hand, was a sleek, black example of feline beauty; her coat glossy and smooth, her eyes a liquid amber that glowed green at night and never ever missed a thing. Minou was not a name she would have chosen for herself, but she put up with it because she had a passing affection for the woman. As she eyed the dusty alley and the broken windows on the shop, she despaired internally of the woman's wilfulness. If she had words, she would have said, "*Merde*[2]!"

"*Alors*, Minou, nothing a lick of paint couldn't solve. A few hours, and some — what do they call it — elbow grease? That should do it! Come now, *ma choupette*[3], you have seen me do it before, and you know I am more than capable of it."

Minou had been witness to the woman's many forays into the business of love, and frankly, could understand none of it. She herself was of the opinion that mating of any kind was an unnecessary pastime that provided momentary pleasure and little else. Therefore, she abstained. She had seen many an alley cat fall foul of the disease called *amour* and had long decided to side-step the entire business altogether.

On this dusty road, close to midnight, the woman and the cat looked at the little shop with varying degrees of interest.

Ottilie, the woman, only saw potential, while Minou, the cat, saw another month or two of dodging the pesky human species once again. "*Magnifique*[4]," thought one. "*Terrible*," thought the other.

And so the adventure began.

"Elodie, *regarde*[5]! Is this a new place? I have never seen it before."

The two friends stood before the pink confection of a café, rather unimaginatively named *Café L'amour*. The red hearts that surrounded the name left no doubt as to the intent of the enterprise.

"Nor have I," the gamine girl named Elodie commented softly, astonishment tingeing the edges of her words. Her large blue eyes took in the pink walls, the white heart-shaped chairs and tables, the entire backdrop of pink and white roses, and the smell of baking that emanated from within.

"I walked past just the other day," Charlotte, the long-limbed brunette said, "I could've sworn this did not exist then."

"You couldn't possibly have missed this!" Elodie agreed.

"Let's go in. We were planning to get our *café au lait*[6] at Francois's anyway."

"*Oui*[7], something smells wonderful, and my stomach has just growled."

"I heard it, *cherie*[8]!" Charlotte laughed, opening the door to the establishment.

Inside, a cloud of vanilla engulfed them. Couples sat at tables sipping on their coffees, eating heart-shaped cakes and gazing lovingly into each other's eyes.

"*Mon Dieu*[9]! Have we wandered onto a film shoot?" Charlotte looked around in disbelief. "*Mais non*[10], it is Valentine's Day today. I had completely forgotten!" Then she looked at Elodie's face and took her hand. "I am so sorry! I do not know what I was thinking... Perhaps we go somewhere else?"

Elodie shook her head, walking towards the display of cakes and pastries.

"It is okay," she smiled sadly, "I am okay."

The large woman behind the counter was busy serving another man, so they waited their turn. Suddenly a cat jumped down from the ledge which housed multiple red heart-shaped boxes of chocolate, and rubbed itself against Elodie's leg.

"Ah, what a beautiful cat!" She bent down to stroke its back.

"Her name is Minou, and I am Ottilie." The large lady smiled at Elodie, her gaze piercing. "Welcome to *Café L'amour*."

"We have never seen you here before?" Charlotte enquired.

"That is because we were never here before. I go where my services are required."

"Your services?"

"My cakes, my bakes." Ottilie kept looking at Elodie while addressing Charlotte. Uncomfortable, Elodie focussed on the cat purring at her feet.

"Then what would you recommend to two friends meeting up after a long time?"

"Aha! For that, two *chocolat chaud*[11] and my special pistachio *financiers*[12]."

"Bon! That is what we will have then. And no, Elodie, I am paying this time. Like we agreed, *ça va*[13]?"

Once seated at the table with their drinks and cakes, Charlotte reached over and took Elodie's hand in hers.

"You have been avoiding me!"

"No, no, that is not true."

"Did you think I would not remember?"

Elodie looked down at her lap.

"Not that. Too many people remember, and it hurts me more that they do."

"Cherie, it has been two years. Perhaps it is time to move on?"

Elodie's big blue eyes filled with tears.

"How?" She whispered.

"So that is the one then, Minou?"

The cat licked its paw in response while the woman contemplated the sunset from the window of her café. The two girls had been striking in different ways. Charlotte had the brittle confidence of one who had bounced back from the many punches life had thrown at her, but it was Elodie that Minou had picked. What anguish lay behind those beautiful eyes and that heart-shaped face?

They had left just a few crumbs of the *financiers* on their plates, Ottilie observed as she cleared up after them. The cups were nearly empty too. Those two would be back, of that she was sure.

Barely twenty-four hours prior, Ottilie and Minou had walked the streets of Paris, looking for the ideal spot. There was sadness that lingered in many places, but there was also laughter, joy and acceptance.

"*Non*[14]," Ottilie would mouth, and Minou would move on, sighing internally.

At nearly midnight, they'd chanced upon a cobble-stoned street lined by a wall of ivy just off Boulevard Saint-Germain. Minou had led the way, with Ottilie following closely on her heels.

From grocery stores, food stalls, cheese shops and gelato stands, the street had everything, except a café. There was an aura of disrepair and brokenness, neglect and afterthought that hung in the air. The paint was peeling on the facades, the stands more than just a little worse for the wear.

"It is perfect, Minou!" Ottilie had clapped her hands together, standing in front of the locked shop.

Minou had watched the woman, unblinking, as she'd cogitated over her decision, pacing back and forth, back and forth.

At one point, a drunk had knocked into her.

"*Pardon!*" He'd apologised to the lamppost, staggering away, spotting neither the woman nor the cat. They were invisible, of course.

"Think," said Ottilie, recovering from the drunken bump, "Think of what we could do here!"

Yes, thought Minou, think of the giant meringue you will create once again. All that pink.

"You mock me, Minou! Pink is the colour of romance, and it has never failed me before..."

That much was true. In all their travels, in whichever part of France they found themselves in, Ottilie's pink cafés had done what not even the perfect champagne and caviar could.

"Now, if we are in agreement, I will place my spell upon the place. For the next month or so, this shop will appear as this to those who do not require my services. But, for those who do, *alors!* They will be enchanted, drawn in by the lure of my incomparable bakes, by the promise of healing *leurs coeurs*[15]."

Not to mention the vanity of the endeavour, thought Minou, flicking her tail from side to side.

"*Tu es une cynique*[16], Minou!"

Having slipped in noiselessly, the pair of them navigated the interior of the dusty shop. Broken furniture was stacked in a corner, a single lightbulb illuminating the acres of dust that covered everything. A barber-shop in its previous life, the mirrors that lined one wall had dark and blotchy spots on their surfaces. Faded linoleum on the floor and a cracked washbasin on the back wall completed the inventory.

"This had many happy customers once, Minou! You may not believe that looking at it now, but *presque certainement*[17]. It will once again be a cheerful place. Now, to work."

With that, Ottilie set about transforming the interior of the shop into the café that Elodie and Charlotte would visit the following day.

Meanwhile, in a different part of the city, not too far away from the café, Elodie woke up to the sound of coughing. Slipping out of her bed, she made her way into the next bedroom. Picking up the glass of water on the bedside table, she brought it to the lips of the old man even as she propped him against the headboard.

"Oh, Papa!" She looked at the gaunt face of her once handsome and full-of-life father, and allowed herself the luxury of a few tears. How difficult it was still to accept the reality of his decline. Slurred speech, incontinence, and incomprehension were the remnants of a stroke that had felled her Papa. Today, he was a mere shadow of himself. So, she wept softly for a bit, and then taking her handkerchief wiped his mouth and her own tears.

Settling him back into the pillows, she pulled the covers up to his chin and kissed him softly, before making her way back to bed. But sleep, ah, that was an elusive thing.

Lying in the night's stillness, Elodie contemplated her future. She was nearly thirty, self-employed and a carer for her father. Her choices had left her with very few friends, and her responsibilities with very little time to communicate with the ones that remained. Perhaps it was time to reach out to the few that still kept in touch. How long could she grieve for a beautiful past, and a never-to-be future?

Picking up her phone, she texted Charlotte.

"Yes, let us meet at Francois's tomorrow. Same time as before."

How was she to know that this would be the beginning of something special?

The people that sat in the café as Charlotte and Elodie peered in were not merely for effect. They had wandered in, just as Ottilie had predicted, enchanted by the promise of something that could not be articulated. Couples who were halfway to falling in love or halfway to falling out of love, singletons with a sweet tooth, an elderly widower, a group of spinsters - all needing or missing love from their lives.

Now, of course, they had love of other sorts. Whether that was the love of a child or a sibling, or even that of a pet. What they did not have was romantic love. That which love stories are made of. The sort of love that had a dashing suitor or a beautiful maiden in need of rescuing. Or just a person who might love them for themselves.

For most people who wandered into this bright and pretty cakery, a little longing still lingered in a corner of their hearts, even while life had taken the sheen off the tales they had grown up listening to. In actual fact, many of them were jaded, cynical even. Fairy tales? Pah! *Quelle stupidité!*[18]

Yet, even under those harsh exteriors, there still beat the tiniest tremor of hope. One that signalled that love might just come their way once, or once again.

Ottilie wove her way through them, her large person surprisingly light on her feet, glancing at Minou from time to time.

A young man held onto his lover's hands, beseeching her not to leave.

Ottilie raised her eyebrows at Minou, even as she placed the delicate *macarons*[19] in front of them. The cat stared down from her perch, unblinking.

Not them, then.

An elderly gentleman sat sipping on his coffee, taking a small bite of his *mille-feuille*[20].

Not him either.

The group of women who sat gossiping together, not a wedding ring between them. Aha! Here she espied a chance.

But no, Minou remained fixed in her place.

From one table to the next, she glided like a ship, each time hoping that Minou would choose the one. But it was not to be.

Hence, she retreated to the kitchen mid-morning, disappointed. Maybe today was not the day, even though it was the one day that had never failed her. A day of love, when the most deserving hearts presented themselves, ready for her ministrations.

Then she heard the two girls approach the display of cakes. Almost immediately Minou jumped down gracefully, weaving herself between the legs of the little one, a petite blonde with big blue eyes and the skittishness of a colt. As always, Minou had chosen well.

"And it is quite a ridiculous place, Papa. You would not believe how pink it is! But the cakes are so delicious. I have never eaten a better *financier* in my entire life." Elodie rhapsodised while spooning the soup into her father's mouth, wiping the edges of his mouth with the napkin. She chatted on, not sure how much he understood or retained, but that had never been the point, anyway.

After lunch, she wheeled his chair to the south-west window of their apartment, where the afternoon rays would lull him into a nap, while she worked alongside on her illustrations. Placing him in the exact same spot where he could view the goings-on of the street below, she covered his knees with a blanket and returned to her chair.

The publisher's secretary had been extremely rude to her the last time, pushing to bring forward the initial deadline. If it were not for the books themselves, she would have quit this job. But the stories, ah! They were mesmerising. If she had had any children, it would be these books she would have bought them. G.G. Boucher had the knack of speaking to the young, and the fact that the publisher wanted Elodie's illustrations to accompany these wonderful tales gladdened her heart.

As she bent over her work, her fingers brought alive the characters of the book, filling in the details of the children's outfits, adding colour to the initial sketches, painting the backgrounds of the fictional world. She had the brief from the publisher's art director, but here and there, she veered off, adding her own little touches, hoping that the writer would appreciate her vision just as much as Elodie appreciated the stories.

Soon, the first few sketches were complete, and Elodie realised that the afternoon light had softened to an evening glow. Her father sat in his wheelchair watching her.

"*Je suis désolée*[21], Papa! I lost track of time." She jumped up, taking hold of the handles of the wheelchair and rushing him towards the bathroom.

That night, after dinner and putting her father to bed, Elodie stood by the same window, a glass of wine in her hand. The pink café floated into her mind again. It made her smile. Tomorrow she would pay it another visit and bring home a pistachio *financier* for Papa too.

Two years ago, a few streets away, there had been a catastrophic accident that had robbed Elodie of a wonderful fiancé, a man by the name of André. Annoyed at being stood up on Valentine's Day, furious that all her texts and calls had gone unanswered, she had stomped home from the restaurant in a rage. Papa had answered the door, enveloping her in a hug before she could understand the stricken look on his face. How soon after had he suffered the stroke? The details of that time blurred in her mind. It just seemed to be a saga of pain and tears, hospitals and funerals, and a huge void where there had once been love and companionship.

In the years since, Elodie had buried herself in work and in caring for her father. Occasionally she would venture out to meet a friend, but the guilt of leaving her poor father alone at home tainted those few stolen hours. As for dating, who would want her and her responsibilities? That is, if her heart ever mended enough for her to give it to anyone else. André had been everything, and when he died, everything had ended.

Elodie blew on her coffee. This time, the large lady (Ottilie, was that the name?) had insisted that she try the chocolate eclair. The *choux* [22]pastry was exactly right, with the perfect softness and bite, the *crème pâtissière* [23]oozing out ever so slightly as she used her fork to cut another bite, the glaze of chocolate sticking to the fingers of her fork even as she deposited the delicious mouthful between her lips. She closed her eyes to appreciate the confluence of flavours - the bitterness of the coffee, the sweetness of the chocolate and the silkiness of the pastry.

"It is good, *non*?"

"Mmmm..." Elodie agreed, her mouth still full.

"Another *café*?"

"*Pourquoi pas*[24]?" Why not indeed, thought Elodie as she smiled up at Ottilie. It had been a while since she'd been in a place as unabashedly happy as this. And once one looked past the over-the-top décor, there was a sweet charm and an unaffected joy to be sitting in the centre of a pink marshmallow.

"Your friend did not come this time?"

"Ah, no. This time I wanted to enjoy this place by myself. Your cakes and pastries are really extremely delicious. I would like to buy some to take back home."

"*Bien sûr!*[25] But they are best enjoyed fresh, and in here." With that, Ottilie moved away to wait on another table.

Elodie looked around her with interest. Who would have thought such a place could exist on a street like this? And just what sorts of people stumbled across it like she had? They were not tourists, that was certain. More like Parisiens unexpectedly finding themselves in a strange part of town.

A *grande dame*[26] who held a cigarette holder with an unlit cigarette in it, one eye on the newspaper and another on the goings-on around her. The newly married couple who sulked in a corner after their first marital spat. Two giddy teenagers who repeatedly kissed, devouring each other with an intensity and hunger that was the domain of youth. Single women who sat at tables, scrolling through their phones or flicking through magazines while nursing their umpteenth cup of coffee, while single men who eyed them from their own tables wondered just how to make the first move.

Elodie absorbed it all, knowing she would transfer this tableau to a sketch as soon as she got home. Just then her phone buzzed.

"Mademoiselle Aubert?"

"*Oui?*[27]"

"It's Jeanine Durand. How are you getting on with the illustrations? The deadline is only a week away."

The infuriating secretary! Elodie had completely forgotten about the call, pushing it to the back of her mind as an unpleasant chore that one procrastinated on indefinitely.

"I have the first few chapters ready."

"First few? Then you are not even halfway there?"

Elodie exhaled, all joy from her surroundings, the coffee and the pastry evaporating instantly.

"Like I explained Madame Durand, I cannot rush this work. After your art director signed off on the initial sketches, we agreed that I would have a minimum of four weeks. Now, you are intent on bringing forward the deadline, but I can only work as fast as I can."

There was complete silence for a minute, and then the line disconnected.

"*Allo?*" Elodie spoke into her phone, perplexed.

"Your *café*," Ottilie placed the cup in front of Elodie. "Are you all right?"

"Yes, I'm... it's... just work..."

"But it's never 'just work', is it? Our work is so much a part of our lives, *non*? For you, for me, and for so many people, it is never 'just work'. Tell me, what is bothering you?"

And suddenly Elodie found herself confiding in the older woman, all her concerns spilling out of her in a rush. Her love of her work that was being barrelled over for some odd reason by a woman she'd never met.

"So, this Madame Durand has been calling you repeatedly and moving the deadline all the time?"

Ottilie had seated herself on the other chair and was regarding her with a serious expression.

"*Oui.*"

"And you have not spoken to the publisher, the art director, or even the author in the past few weeks?"

"No, I have not." Elodie's brow furrowed. "Nearly all my communication has been through Madame Durand."

"Well," Ottilie looked at her, "Perhaps it is time for you to go straight to... *la source* ?"

"You mean, go to the office?"

"*Pourquoi pas*?" Ottilie beamed at her, and all at once, it became clear to Elodie that that was exactly what she would do. Why ever not?

A little after Elodie had left, and Ottilie sat behind the counter taking a nibble out of her croissant during a lull in the café's busy morning, Minou appeared out of nowhere, and sat right in front of her.

"Now, do not regard me in that fashion. I have left a bowl of milk for you in the corner, but all you want is *pâté!*[28] You will get fat, Minou."

The cat almost smirked at that, and stung, Ottilie retorted, "I am not twenty anymore! How can you expect me to be as slim as a ballerina, eh?"

In response, Minou took a few steps towards the bowl, and lapped up all the milk, not a drop lingering on her black whiskers.

"*Bonne fille*[29]!" Ottilie smiled. "Now listen to what I have done..."

❦

After the split of the famous Houy publishing house, Bernard Dubois, maverick co-founder and former editor of Houy, launched Le Fauteuil in the summer of 2018. Dubois was interested in the sensibility of the artist and published any text that touched him enough. For him, publishing a book meant defending it in all its strangeness and uniqueness. It was no wonder that under the auspices of his publishing house, categories such as French fiction, foreign fiction and illustrated books flourished like nowhere else.

Many publishing houses had rejected G.G. Boucher's strange tales for children before they found a refuge at Le Fauteuil. The first book had become such a household name that Dubois himself had declared that Boucher's sweet but amateurish illustrations would no longer suffice. In a search that had seen thousands of submissions from many talented illustrators, Dubois and Boucher had settled on Mademoiselle Aubert's fanciful sketches. Where others had been too potent, hers were quiet to the point of being nearly invisible, until you found yourself in their thrall. Where other colours screamed for notice, her pale watercolours wove a silent magical spell on the reader; where other more distinctive styles nearly overpowered the dream-like text of the stories, Aubert's ethereal drawings pulled one in deeper, complementing the surreal chimerical writings of Boucher. It was a match made in Heaven, except for one tiny detail.

Madame Durand.

For nearly two years, Madame Durand had been trying to get her autistic nephew employed. Having promised her late sister that she would always look out for him, she had tried getting him many a job. But his personality traits rendered him all but unemployable. Pierre had no desire to work with other humans. His only interest lay in sketching the birds that frequented his windowsill at the apartment he shared with his aunt. Those he drew beautifully, each feather sketched with such precision that the bird seemed to come alive on the page. When Madame Durand realised her nephew was unusually talented in this arena, she made it her mission to have him commissioned the illustrator for the new author making waves: G.G. Boucher.

She was all but certain that with a little manipulation and a lot of direction, Pierre could turn his attention to creating artwork for Boucher's new book. She had seen both Dubois and Boucher pause at his drawings (the ones she'd slipped into the pile without their knowledge) amongst the many they had perused, commenting on the use of colour and light. If it hadn't been for that damned girl, she would have had that contract signed, sealed and delivered to Pierre by now!

Anyhow, all was not lost. If she pressured her enough, Mademoiselle Aubert was bound to chuck it all in. Just the result she was hoping for. After all, a reclusive illustrator, clearly anti-social (for she refused to come in person to sign the contract) could only be pushed so far before she snapped. People like her would always get more chances in life. People like her poor Pierre hardly would.

"The thing is Minou, that every single *personne* [30]is deserving of love," Ottilie said, as she waved her hands around the kitchen, creating more culinary delights out of thin air. "To live a life without it, why, that is a crime and a punishment!"

Minou licked her paw.

"So, why not give everyone love? Well, if it was in my power, of course I would! But you see, Minou, we all carry invisible suitcases around with us. They are filled with the weight of our experiences — hurt, betrayal, anger and sadness are far heavier than hope and joy. We drag these cases around, unknowingly weighing ourselves down and allowing so many opportunities for love to pass us by because we are burdened. *Oui*, burdened!"

Ottilie contemplated the room.

"Our minds are full, so full of all the *négatif* [31], that we cannot contemplate the good without believing it to be untrue. In such an atmosphere, my powers are limited to those who will still allow their hearts to be opened, despite all the sadness that lives within them. It is these that we seek, is it not, my Minou? And when we find them, ah! What a sense of discovery, of potential..." She smiled. "Then I come into my own, using the one thing I'm good at..."

Minou sniffed the air.

"No, not baking! Although *je suis trop talentueuse*[32]. But if I have to use my talent for anything, it is most heartening to use it in bringing love into someone's life. So, to that end, I have sent Elodie on a mission with a box of pistachio *financiers*. There is a separate one for her Papa. But first, she must sweeten the opposition."

The petite girl who was struggling with the door and a large box looked like she would get blown away by the wind any minute. Gérard stepped forward to pull the door open for her. With a sweet smile, she thanked him politely before stepping into the small lobby of the offices of Le Fauteuil. Something in the enormous pink heart-shaped box she was carrying smelled delicious.

"*Excusez-moi,*[33] but what is that you have in your hands?"

"This?" She looked startled. "Oh, just some cakes from a new café near my house. *Délicieux*[34]!"

Gérard made a mental note to visit this new café, internally filing away the name he'd spotted on the box as he walked into the elevator with the pretty young woman. He wondered whom she was visiting here. Perhaps her father?

Since the desk at the lobby had been unmanned, neither of them had needed to declare whom they were here to see. So when they both alighted at the same floor, Gérard laughed and held the door open once again, letting her exit the elevator first.

Something about this gamine girl was intriguing. She was pretty, no doubt, but it was those big, blue eyes that seemed to hold many secrets which had caught his attention. In the two-minute ride up, he'd tried to think of conversational gambits and come up short. She had been content with the silence.

As he walked behind her now, he observed the little grey jacket and red knee-length kick-flare skirt she wore. Her legs were shapely and slim, but the ankles, dainty in their black stockings, seemed particularly beautiful to him. Her perfume reminded him of a delicate rose, only just coming into bloom. That, mixed with whatever she was carrying in the box, pulled him magnetically behind her. Had she been walking through the doorway to Hell, he would have followed her in.

It may not have been Hell, but the harridan that sat behind the desk could have burnt them both alive with the look she directed at them.

"Who sent you up?" She growled.

The girl wilted visibly.

"I... uh..."

"Is Bernard in?" Gérard deflected quickly, hoping to turn the harridan's ire towards himself and away from the girl.

"Is Madame Durand in?" The girl said at the same time.

They both stopped and looked at each other.

"Monsieur Dubois is in a meeting, and I am Madame Durand." She glared at them. Then her brow wrinkled as she looked at Gérard. "Aren't you...?"

But before she could say anything, the elegant sprite by his side had whisked the cover of the box open, and an incredible aroma rose in the air.

"Madame Durand, for our misunderstanding earlier today, I have brought you and Monsieur Dubois some pistachio *financiers*."

Gérard's mouth fairly salivated. He'd always had a sweet tooth, but even if he hadn't, there was something about these little cakes that it was all he could do to not reach out and pop one into his mouth there and then. Maybe it was a sentiment that was shared by Madame Durand, because her entire body seemed to relax as she eyed the treats in the box.

"And a stroke of genius that was too, Minou!" Ottilie crossed her legs at her ankles and clasped her hands. For a brief while she had shut the café by making it invisible to all. She was exhausted from all the plotting and planning, and just needed a moment to relax.

People often spoke about reading tea leaves in cups, but no one ever talked about the work involved in reading the crumbs off a plate.

Much, much harder! For one thing, she'd gotten the two plates in a muddle, and ended up reading Charlotte's crumbs first.

"*Mon Dieu!*" She'd exclaimed at the parade of boyfriends, each more unsavoury than the last, until she'd realised that Charlotte was more than capable of handling the affairs of the heart. It was then that she'd turned her attention to Elodie's crumbs.

"Now there was a real tragedy, Minou. Childhood sweethearts about to marry, and then on Valentine's Day no less, that he was in a collision. Our poor Elodie's heart shattered, her dreams over like so." She snapped her fingers, waking Minou from her nap. "But then I spied something in those crumbs... A ray of hope, *cherie*. Or, perhaps it was the butter, but *qui s'en soucie*[35]! Who cares? It was enough, more than enough. I knew then that I could find love for this girl. In fact, it is right there, right in front of her. But she still has to spot it..."

Minou yawned, curled up into a ball, and promptly fell asleep once again.

"You are welcome to have some too," Elodie offered the man who had followed her into the office. There was something instantly likeable about him, something that reminded her of André, although he was much older. Greying at the temples, bespectacled, and wearing an old Tweed jacket, he was nowhere near as suavely handsome as André had been. But for all that, she'd felt a warm glow as his gaze had rested upon her in the elevator.

For the first time in two years, her heart had unclenched. This man, of whom she knew nothing, felt like a safe harbour; a place where she could rest her weary bones, where she could be understood and be taken care of.

As her blue eyes met his green ones, she felt a jolt of recognition. It was as though André was smiling at her from behind the glasses, whispering, "*Ma douce*[36]..."

Then Madame Durand brought her back to earth by noisily clearing her throat and offering them both coffee, which they readily accepted.

The *financiers* worked their magic, exactly as Ottilie had predicted, and Madame Durand smiled on her more benevolently. Even as the man excused himself to use the washroom, she ushered Elodie to a side and agreed that there would be no more bringing forward of the deadline, and that they must never refer to it again. Then she launched into an explanation about someone called Pierre, turned red, cut herself off and took another bite of the *financier*, before choking on it most dramatically.

The man returned to rescue the situation by slapping her heartily on the back, while Elodie rushed to get her a glass of water. In all the hubbub, the coffees were entirely forgotten.

When the clock struck noon, Elodie remembered Papa's lunch, and ran out of the office much like Cinderella with no glass slippers to leave behind.

It was later that night that she realised she hadn't even got the man's name.

Charlotte eyed the cakes behind the glass counter. The woman serving them seemed a bit out of sorts, and the cat was nowhere to be seen.

"No more pistachio *financiers*?"

"*Alors!* Each morning there is a queue that stretches around the corner. I open at 9 a.m., and by 9:15, we are sold out."

"Well, that's good for business, *non*?"

"Not my sort of business." The woman looked overwrought, and it was not even noon yet.

"Come and sit down here," Charlotte guided the woman out from behind the stall, ignoring all the curious looks being thrown their way. Somehow, since her last visit with Elodie a month ago, the café seemed to have lost a bit of its lustre. It seemed a little less pink and a lot more subdued. Quite like its proprietor.

"You seem to be doing well, so why are you upset? Oh, and by the way, my name is Charlotte."

"*Je sais*[37]." The woman shrugged.

But how could she possibly know? Unless she'd eavesdropped on their conversation... But even so, after all this time?

"And you are?" Charlotte probed.

"A failure!" She wrung her hands while making the declaration.

"I mean, your name?"

"Ah! Ottilie." She grimaced.

"*Bon*[38], Ottilie. Now, I'm not sure why I am sitting here trying to counsel you when I should be sipping on my coffee and biting into a pastry, but here we go. What is the problem?"

"There is a time limit on these sorts of things. A month is too much! By now, it should have been done. *Tout indiqait que ce serait fait*[39]... and now, Minou is missing too!"

The woman was clearly bonkers - *dingue*[40]! But Charlotte kept a straight face.

"Is Minou the cat?"

"*Oui!*" Ottilie's distress was clear. "She has never left me like this before. Two days... two entire days!"

But Minou was no ordinary cat. When Elodie had failed to return to the café, and nor had her love life magically materialised, Ottilie had taken to muttering curses under her breath. How, she'd questioned Minou, were so many customers turning up day after day, asking for her pistachio *financiers*? And where was her pet project? What could have gone so wrong with her plan? She had seen it all in the crumbs, but had she misread the signs? Had she gotten it all horribly, terribly, completely wrong? Was she getting too old for this business? Was it time for her to retire?

Finally, bored senseless by all of Ottilie's complaints and questions, Minou had taken things into her own hands. Alley after alley, she'd wandered in search of the elusive girl. She'd jumped over walls and scaled fences, peered in through windows, and nearly fallen through a chimney — until she'd come across an old man who stared at her from a window, his gaze as unblinking as her own. And a girl trying to spoon soup into his mouth.

. . .

For, nearly a month ago, as Elodie had gotten home almost a half hour later than expected, her Papa had suffered another stroke. Rushing him to hospital, she had vowed never ever to leave his side again. Between sobs, she'd held his hand and prayed hard for him to live. Forgetting everything — the café, the cakes, Madame Durand, the lovely man in the office — she'd devoted herself to the one person who had never failed her or given up on her. Day and night she'd tended to him, forgetting her work, ignoring the phone calls and the doorbell ringing, and focussed on bringing her Papa back to normality.

Minou took it all in, stretching out in the sunshine. Ah, this would take all her feline wiles, and then some!

Meanwhile, Gérard visited the café daily, hoping to run into the beautiful girl again. Upon pressing her, Madame Durand had revealed that her name was Elodie, but had turned tight-lipped after that, refusing to give out any more details. With only the box as his clue, he turned up every day at the café, trying different times but with no luck. He was yet to run into the young woman who had stolen his heart so very quickly. Alongside was the disappointment of not getting to taste the pistachio *financier* once more. It remained perpetually sold out.

The eccentric owner of the café had given him a sharp glance when, three days in a row, he'd asked for one. She jangled her bracelets at him and asked, "Where did you find out about my *financiers* from?"

"Uh..." Intimidated by her fierce scowl, he'd muttered some gibberish about a friend, and she'd stomped off, clearly dissatisfied by his answer.

Now, she seemed to be sitting and weeping, wringing her hands and talking to a striking brunette over in the corner of the café. If not for her apparent distress, he might have gathered up the courage to ask about a petite blonde customer of hers.

He sighed into his coffee. What a fool he'd been! A *coup de foudre* [41]— did he really believe in love at first sight? At his age?

For nearly forty-five years of his life, love had eluded him. Oh, it had danced around him many times, inviting him to taste of its pleasures. But each instance had proven to be a mirage. He was not an easy man to understand, and the only people who were truly at ease in his company were under the age of twelve. Which is why he spent more time in the company of his nieces and nephews than he did with their parents. It was their outlook on life that fascinated him — their ability to dream, their fantasies untainted by cynicism, their belief in something bigger than themselves and this world they inhabited.

Enough! It was time to get back to the books. A new story that was brewing in his mind had been relegated to the background while he searched for the girl. Now that the search had proven to be *le fiasco* [42], it was prudent to accept defeat and head home, never to return to this ridiculous pink atrocity of an establishment. Why, even a character in his book would not set foot in such a place! And yet, his gaze lingered on the hearts, the flowers and the cakes, wishing things could be different.

He looked at the notes he'd been making and tucked them carefully into his book. A few examples of Aubert's drawings were tucked in alongside. He hoped to make an acquaintance of the illustrator someday, even if it was just to say 'bravo'! How could someone he had never met be so sympathetic to his vision? He hoped someday he would get a chance to find out. But for now, it was time to give up on this silly obsession.

Gérard stood up quickly, knocking over his book accidentally, spilling the notes and illustrations on the floor. The door to the café opened at exactly the same moment, allowing in a blast of air and swirling the sheets of paper up into the wind. He tried to catch them, but another gust blew a sheet onto the face of the girl standing at the door. The black cat she was holding let out an indignant mew and dropped out of her hands, making its way smoothly across the floor to the large lady who stood up just as suddenly.

"Minou!" She screamed in delight.

The brunette turned towards the door and let out a little yelp of recognition.

"Elodie!"

But neither the man nor the girl at the door noticed her.

G.G. Boucher and Elodie Aubert had eyes only for each other.

The woman and the cat looked at one another.

"Our job here is done, Minou. It is time to move on." Ottilie declared, patting the bag that hung on her side, which looked even more threadbare than before.

The cat purred contentedly.

The store had gone back to being what it was. The street was still as dismal as before, but a tiny spark of love danced near the lamp-post, a remnant of the joy that had ignited in this very spot that morning.

The drunk once again knocked into the woman, looked askance at the lamppost and backed away hurriedly, making a sign of the cross on his chest, vowing never to walk on this street again.

As the woman and the cat melted away, the little spark still danced its little jig in front of the run-down shop. Love, once ignited, was hard to extinguish. So it danced its merry dance, for Elodie and Gérard, for broken hearts and mended hearts, for those looking for love and those fortunate enough to have it.

It danced for lovers everywhere.

~

2

____

OSTERHASE

I first saw him when I was nine. Oma [1] had hidden the Easter eggs in her vast garden, and I searched for them half-heartedly. More for the sake of Antje, my younger sister. I was never fond of chocolate, and that, I suppose, was yet another reason I was considered 'odd' by my peers.

Only Opa [2] understood my aversion to chocolate, and then later, to all things religious. He was an atheist too. But back then, he daren't have mentioned it to Oma, who was fiercely religious, dragging us to church for Sunday Service, Easter, Midnight Mass and any other occasion that required worship or penitence.

But that chilly April morning, when dew still rested on the grass, and the crocuses were making their way up through the soil, worship was the farthest thing from our minds. Oma was baking an *Oster-lamm* [3] in the kitchen, and the smell of vanilla and powdered sugar infiltrated the air much like the pollen that made Opa sneeze.

We were to have roast lamb, potatoes and red cabbage for lunch. Another Easter tradition at our grandparents' house. Mutti [4] and Papa were away on their annual vacation, leaving us in their care, and unlike Antje, I hadn't cried this time. In the past year I had understood that my grandparents were old, and that this time with them was precious. It was after Hans had lost his grandfather to a heart attack and come to school with swollen eyes that I had vowed to never complain about being left behind. Antje was still too young to understand this, and despite having shed a bucket-load of tears, she had cheered up immediately upon being offered a Ritter Sport. Ah, the simplicity of being five.

We had attended Easter service at the festively decorated church that morning. Antje had yawned loudly the entire time, and I'd had to remind her in a hushed whisper that the *Osterhase*[5] wouldn't leave her any eggs if she carried on this way. She'd bitten her lip for the rest of the service, suppressing any further yawns.

But now, as we hunted for the eggs, I could see her getting visibly distressed.

"Stefan, *es gibt keine Eier*[6]?"

"Of course there are eggs! We have not looked hard enough..."

This was Opa's doing, that was for certain. Each year he made it harder, wanting to challenge me. A game of wits, he called it, forgetting that Antje was not interested in such games. Her only motivation was to stuff as much chocolate as she could into her mouth, and then create a necklace out of all the foil wrappers.

I looked up at the sky. It was getting brighter as the sun climbed up through the clouds, evaporating the dew on the grass. A pale sunshine descended upon the garden, setting off the bright colours of the decorative eggs Oma had hung upon the branches. Years later, when I found one such egg nestling in a box in the attic, I wondered what had happened to the rest. But by then, almost everything in my life had gone awry, and a few lost eggs were the least of my problems.

Oma and Opa were the generation that had survived the Second World War. They had been mere children when Germany had surrendered, but the shame of the generation before hung over them. They were good people, my grandparents, but a nation's guilt is always assumed by its inhabitants. So they worked hard and kept to their patch of land on the outskirts of Köln, having no ambition except to live a quiet existence.

Opa was a twenty-year-old university student when he met Oma in Bonn. She was working at a local haberdashery, selling buttons, zippers, threads and such like. Opa had split his trousers, and the rest, he always laughed as he said this, "was history". At nine, I did not understand what that meant. At any rate, to me everything associated with them had a whiff of history to it. From the old-fashioned bedspread in our room to the numerous traditions that Oma inflicted upon us, and the many varied and colourful eggs that danced upon the branches of the trees this morning.

"Stefan, *sich beeilen*[7]!"

Antje was hurrying me along, impatient to find the chocolate eggs. At five, she believed in the Easter Bunny and Father Christmas, just as much as she believed in fairies and elves. I believed in very little.

We'd looked in all the usual places—behind the bushes and shrubs, in the hollow of the old oak tree, even peeked in through the window of the garden shed—but so far there was no sign of them.

Normally there would be two baskets, one lined with pink tissue and filled with all the chocolates that Antje loved, and the other lined with blue and filled with the chocolate I pretended to love. Invariably those ended up with Antje too.

Now, with a trembling lip she stood near the tree, perilously close to tears. Hastily, I pulled out the two scraps of paper that Opa had put the clues on.

"Antje, wait! Let's go over these again. Maybe we missed something..."

She sniffed and nodded, coming over to examine the scraps with me. On Antje's he'd drawn a chicken, a feather, and a hat. On mine, he'd written the numbers "8 5 4".

"I suggest we split up. You take the left side of the garden and I'll take the right."

"But where do I find the chicken?"

"Maybe it's not the chicken you need to start with. Maybe start by finding the feather or the hat. Opa wouldn't make it too difficult for you. You're only a little girl."

She cheered up visibly, giving me a gap-toothed smile. Then she slipped the clue into the pocket of her red gingham dress and skipped away, her blonde curls bouncing.

I unfolded my paper and studied the numbers again. What could they mean? Were they a birth date? But whose? None of us were born in August, May or April. What if I added the numbers? Hmmm. 17. What significance did that have?

I walked towards the right, pondering the clues, knowing that somewhere back in the house, Opa would be chuckling while Oma scolded him for making it too hard for us.

I was still lost in my thoughts when I heard him clear his throat. It didn't register at first. The second time, he cleared it louder, and my head snapped up. I looked straight into his eyes and stopped in my tracks.

All these years later, when I recall our first meeting, I wonder why I didn't scream and run back to the house. How, at the age of nine, the appearance of an enormous rabbit with pink eyes, a waistcoat and a monocle, did not give me any cause for alarm.

"Hello," he said, "My name is Heinrich. You must be Stefan."

I stared at him.

"You have pink eyes."

"*Jawohl*[8]. I am an unusual *Osterhase*."

"You are the Easter Bunny?"

He regarded me solemnly.

"I thought you were a smart boy."

I drew myself up to my full height.

"I am a smart boy, the smartest in my class."

"Then why must you keep stating the obvious?"

That stumped me for a moment.

"Why are you here? And why are you wearing that ridiculous waistcoat?" I countered.

"Now, Stefan, there is no need to be rude. I see that I have injured your pride and I apologise. As for the choice of garment, well, I do not much care for your half-trousers either, but that should not be an obstacle in the way of our friendship, should it?"

I gulped and nodded, suddenly realising that I was in fact talking to a giant rabbit.

"As to why I'm here. It is to help you, of course. The numbers in your hand... You do not know what they mean, but I do."

Then, just as suddenly, he turned and hopped away from me. I stood staring, not sure whether I was dreaming.

"Well, are you coming or not?" He asked over his shoulder.

I stumbled after him, half-hoping that Opa would come looking for me and confront this strange creature. As Heinrich hopped to the end of the garden, I saw that he meant for me to follow him into the woods. Both Antje and I had been expressly forbidden from entering the woods on our own. Even though Opa and Oma had taken us for walks there, letting us collect pine cones or dip our feet in the stream that ran through, we knew never to go there unaccompanied.

Now, this rabbit stood at the periphery of the garden tapping his foot in impatience.

"I... I cannot follow you there. It's forbidden."

"Why?"

Why? How was I to know why?

"Are you a rule-follower or a rule-breaker, Stefan?"

"I don't understand..." I stammered.

"There are two kinds of people in the world. Those who allow other people to tell them what to do, and those who do the telling. Which one are you?"

"You said you'd help me with the numbers!"

"Ah, yes! So I did." Heinrich took off his monocle and cleaned it on the edge of his waistcoat. "Which book were you reading last night?"

My mind flashed back to us sitting around the fireplace. Oma darning a dress, Antje playing with her doll, Opa reading his newspaper, and I re-reading my favourite book of all time - Around the World in Eighty Days by Jules Verne.

"You will need to consult the fourth word of the fifth paragraph of the eighth chapter to find your answer."

My mouth fell open.

Just then I heard Antje calling out.

"Stefan... Stefan..."

I turned to answer her, but when I turned back, he was gone.

She came running up to me, all ruddy-cheeked, holding up her little basket as a prize.

"It was under Opa's hat!" She giggled as she explained how she found the feather stuck to a tree, pointing towards the bush where she found the rooster weather vane, which eventually led her to Opa's large Homburg hat.

"You are a clever girl!" I enthused, still reeling from my strange encounter.

"And where is your basket?" She looked at me while unwrapping her first egg.

"Yes, Antje, be a dear and bring my book out, will you? The clue is in there, but I don't want Opa seeing me just yet."

She obliged me by running towards the house to fetch my book, while I sat under the poplar tree at the edge of our garden and stared into the woods.

Where had he gone? Had I imagined him? There was only one way to find out.

When Antje appeared with my book, I grabbed it from her, uttering a quick "thanks". Flicking through the pages, I arrived at Chapter Eight:

'In Which Passepartout Talks Rather More, Perhaps, Than Is Prudent'

My finger moved swiftly down the page to find paragraph five, alighting upon the fourth word: 'travel'.

Travel?

Opa had never travelled outside of Germany, but he kept a globe in the living room, which he often spun, randomly stopping it and saying, "And this, young Stefan, is where your adventure will begin..."

Thus far, I had been to Nairobi, Guam, The Easter Islands and Bhutan. All in Opa's imagination.

Where was the globe? I hadn't seen it in its usual place this morning, but I had seen it somewhere else.

"Stefan?" Antje looked at me curiously.

"I know where it is!" I sat up excitedly.

The door opened noiselessly, its hinges having been oiled recently. There, in a corner of the garden shed, sat the large blue globe, obscuring the small basket lined with blue tissue and filled with a variety of chocolate eggs.

Both of us were hailed for our cleverness, and fussed over and spoilt for the rest of the holiday. Perhaps that's why I never mentioned Heinrich to my grandparents. But I took to wandering towards the end of the garden daily to peer into the woods, hoping he might reappear. He didn't. Not then. Not for a while.

Having lost Oma to a stroke, Opa insisted on living on his own in his "house of memories". Mutti despaired of him, Antje tried reasoning with him, all to no avail. But I understood. Opa and I had always had an understanding.

After Mutti's divorce from Papa, we moved into a small flat in central Köln. It was on the second floor, with just two small bedrooms, and I took to sleeping on the foldout bed-cum-sofa in the living room to give Antje the privacy she craved at thirteen.

My teenage years were turbulent - filled with alcohol-fuelled rages and marijuana-induced periods of "chilling". I was only a few steps away from sliding towards heroin and crack-cocaine. Maybe that's why Mutti sent me to Opa that Summer.

I had smuggled a few tokes with me, and took care never to smoke in the house. Opa hardly ever drank, and his drink of choice was beer, anyway. So, I drank his vodka, emptying it into my flask and filling the bottle with water, then tucking it back behind all the other dusty bottles of liquor that sat unopened and unused in a small cabinet in the living room.

Opa was in his sixties now, and still an agile, athletic man. Whilst Oma was alive, he'd hardly said anything, letting her do the talking for the both of them. He was still taciturn, but prone to letting slip the occasional wry observation. In my second week at his house, he asked me, "Stefan, *hast du keine freunde*[9]?"

I had friends. There was Hans, the full-time junkie; Ingrid, who blacked-out every night after consuming an entire bottle of wine; and Antje, my younger sister, who adored me despite all my flaws. And believe me, I had many.

"Why?"

"It is just that you call no one, and no one calls you. At your age, I was always out with my friends."

"I prefer my own company."

Opa regarded me from above his glasses.

"Do you remember that last Easter with your Oma?"

I had a vague recollection of eggs hanging off trees, and Opa's clues to find our baskets.

"Not really."

"Well, you must have been nine, and I had made the clues a bit harder that year, even though Oma chastised me for it. But I knew you were smart enough to crack it, and you did. Remember the word?"

Somewhere from the recesses of my mind, an image of a globe swam up to meet me.

"Travel?" I enquired, tentatively.

"Yes, travel." Opa coughed. "You are a young man with brains and ability, and the world at your feet. I want you to do what I couldn't. Don't waste your time or you will live with regret in your later years."

That was the most Opa had spoken to me lately, and I absorbed his words, squirrelling them away to nibble on later.

Wandering through the woods a few days on, I took a deep and delicious drag of my toke, then sat down by the stream, watching the light play flirtatiously upon the water.

Eighteen and no clue what I wanted in life. But that was also the life of my peers. We were all adrift, incapable of shedding our teenage angst, searching for escape or oblivion through any means possible.

Papa had remarried, while Mutti remained stubbornly single.

Antje had adjusted to our half-siblings, happy to visit or stay over in Dusseldorf with Papa's new family. But that was Antje - easygoing, likeable, happy to go with the flow. I had inherited Mutti's intractability.

I leaned my head back against the tree trunk and closed my eyes. A deep fatigue made my limbs ache, and a lassitude filled my body. Was there any point to any of it? I could travel, but wherever I went, I would still encounter sadness, broken families, splintered dreams and death. There was no escaping the human condition.

"So now you are a mere observer?"

The gravelly voice startled me out of my reverie. I opened my eyes to stare right into a pair of pink ones.

"Heinrich?" My voice came out as a croak.

"Indeed."

"But... but... you are an *Osterhase!*"

"I have never denied it."

"Then what are you doing here in August?"

"Do I cease to exist in other months? I am here because you need me."

"Need you? I haven't even thought about you in years."

"And yet, you remembered my name straight away."

"For all I know, you could be a hallucination!" I looked at the rolled-up joint in my hand.

"But you know that I am not." He sat opposite me, still wearing that grey waistcoat, a monocle over his left eye. He seemed utterly at ease in his surroundings, as though he had always belonged in these woods and I was the interloper.

"You wanted me to follow you into the woods last time. What did you want to show me?"

"That can wait. Today I want to ask you something."

"I want to ask you something too."

"Very well, you go first. *Frag mich*[10]!"

"Are you real?"

He looked at me solemnly.

"As real as the sun, the trees, those flowers and you."

"Why should I believe you?"

"You need not. But if you need proof, here, take my monocle. I have another. You can keep it." He handed me the round silver-rimmed monocle and took another one out of his pocket and placed it on his eye.

My fingers rubbed the soft smoothness of the glass over and over, as if to reassure me of the solidity of its state, and perhaps my own mental faculties.

"Why are you here?" My question was tinged with a wonderment, a feeling of somehow being removed from everything; as if watching it all from a safe distance, the boy and rabbit conversing in an utterly normal fashion.

"It's my turn, Stefan." Heinrich's penetrating gaze made me drop my eyes. I nodded mutely.

"I had asked you once what kind of man you planned to be. I ask you again, are you a bystander to your own life? A passive witness, allowing the tides of times to take you where they may?"

A sudden fury blazed through me.

"And who are you to ask me this? A giant rabbit that appears at will and disappears into nowhere! What gives you the right?"

Heinrich regarded me with a gravity that rendered my outburst infantile.

"Life is a precious gift, and yet, look at you. With your rings and piercings, your strange spiked hair and the tattoos on your fingers. Your dependence on chemicals to provide you answers. How you waste your life navel-gazing! Ask your Opa about Samuel."

With that, he hopped away; leaving me bemused, still sitting under the tree, holding his monocle in one hand and the joint in the other.

I wanted to ask Opa straight away, but something held me back. Who was Samuel? I was dying to know. If Samuel did indeed exist, then Opa would want to know how I'd found out about him. How would I explain my encounter with Heinrich to him? I could barely explain it to myself.

I listened to *"Das Omen"* by Mysterious Art on repeat, still sneaking my swigs of vodka but increasingly finding no satisfaction in getting high or drunk.

Heinrich's question plagued me night and day. What kind of man was I turning into? Like Opa, content to just be; or Papa, forever in a hamster wheel of work, money and status?

Looking back, I wonder how Opa put up with a moody teenager in his house all summer. Not only did I barely speak to him, I was untidy and didn't wash for days on end. For a man of his generation, who had worked for over forty years with never a complaint, my behaviour must have seemed bizarre, bordering on the offensive. To his credit, he never upbraided me for it, and instead just left me be and got on with his own daily routine.

Nearly a decade after Oma had passed, Opa found refuge in his little vegetable garden. Every morning, after a hearty breakfast of fruit, a crusty roll spread with *Quark mitt Schnittlauch*[11], two boiled eggs and a glass of *orangensaft*[12], he would retreat to his little patch with a shovel, some gardening gloves, a transistor radio and a mug of Ovaltine. Mid-noon, he would prepare a lunch of Schnitzel with buttered vegetables, and have his lone glass of beer with it. Then he would sit in his rocking chair with a book, often falling asleep a few pages in.

Some days he would go to visit a friend, but most days, he would turn on the television at exactly 6 p.m. and switch it off at exactly 8 p.m.

There was a regularity to his rhythm that I found calming, my own life being totally devoid of any pattern at all.

We spoke little, sometimes grunting at each other if we wished to convey gratitude or affection. But beneath it all, I knew that the love ran deep. Opa was the one constant of my life, a man so upright, so gracious, so devoid of vanity or conceit that subconsciously, I wished to be a source of pride to him. Consciously, however, I did not know how to go about it.

After four weeks of being utterly useless, I felt exhausted with myself. The long days spent in my own company were wearing me down. I was out of tokes, and the remaining vodka stayed in my flask untouched. Heinrich's words still echoed in my mind, but I pushed them away, not knowing the answers to anything.

On a Monday morning I sprang out of bed at 6 a.m., resolving to do something different and be someone different for the rest of my stay. I started with stripping all the linen off the bed and putting it in the washing machine. When Opa emerged from his shower, his eyebrows rose to see me standing outside, towel in hand. I scrubbed myself vigorously with a flannel, washing weeks of grime off my body.

Dressing myself in a clean white T-shirt, I removed the piercing from my ear, combed my hair to one side and sprayed on the cologne Antje had bought me last Christmas.

When I joined Opa at the breakfast table, he looked up at me and smiled.

"Welcome, Stefan. Are you ready for your coffee?"

We worked together in silence at first. Then I started teasing out little details of Opa's family and background. As I knelt in that vegetable patch, handling the soil between my fingers and listening to Opa talk haltingly, a sudden sense of peace descended upon me. I felt at one with the earth and the sky; a child born from the womb of the world and destined to return to it.

In the days that followed, it was as though someone had opened the floodgates. A lifetime's worth of tales spilled from Opa's lips. Often he would pull out a battered old case filled with black-and-white photos, pointing out his mother, his father and his siblings. Some days, he would hand me heavy tomes that excoriated all religions, his atheism becoming increasingly evident as the years advanced. Other days he would talk about Oma with a wistful longing, his companion of a lifetime snatched away too early. No longer just my grandfather, I now saw him as a man with thoughts, feelings and beliefs; a man who was so much more than just a sum of his parts.

"Opa, what made you want to be a carpenter?"

We were sitting together at dinner. I had attempted to make *Eintopf* - a stew that I'd watched Mutti make with leftover ingredients like beans, sausages, lentils and vegetables. Opa had already remarked that it was "*lecker*[13]!" So I was relaxed enough to query him about his choice of profession.

Opa did not answer for a moment or two, but that was not out of character. Unlike other adults who rushed in eager to impart their hard-won wisdom, barely considering the source of or the reason for the enquiry, Opa always took his time to mull over my questions and remarks.

"But you see Stefan," he answered slowly, "I didn't. I wanted to be an airline pilot. I had a great ambition to travel and see the world."

I looked at the sorrow etched on Opa's face and waited for him to proceed. He set his shovel to a side and stood up to stretch. I stood up alongside. The sun was high and beads of sweat trickled down the sides of his face. He looked down at his hands.

"It was my friend Samuel who wanted to be a carpenter."

I shivered in the heat. In all these weeks, Opa had never once mentioned Samuel, and I'd started to think that Heinrich was just a figment of my imagination. But here was Opa, talking of a childhood friend named Samuel.

"... he was so good with his hands, a natural born talent. He could fashion anything out of wood. Somewhere I have a model plane he made me... a Luftwaffe Arado Ar 197... He was so good with his hands..."

"Where is Samuel now?"

"Oh, he died." Opa looked up at the sky.

"How?"

"In the concentration camp at Auschwitz-Birkenau."

～

"What a charming place!" Klara exclaimed, looking around the living room. I looked at it with fresh eyes, and there was an old-fashioned allure to it. All of Oma's flowery patterns were back in fashion, and suddenly the house had taken on a vintage appeal.

In the last ten years, after inheriting the house, I'd hardly visited. It was Antje who came with her family and stayed over the holidays. Every time she asked me why I didn't come, I'd have an excuse handy. "Too busy." "Crazy schedule." "Jet lagged." The reasons rolled off my tongue in a routine litany. The truth was that it was too painful to come to a house divested of its soul.

Opa's death had hit me hard, and I'd nearly abandoned my pilot training to come back to Köln. It was only Mutti's insistence, and her reminders of how Opa had been so proud of me, that had kept me going.

Every time I sat in the cockpit, I whispered to myself, "This is for you, Opa."

Opa would have liked Klara. She was pretty and kind, the sort of girl who would make a family, a girl who could ground me. At thirty-six, I was finally ready to settle down. It was time. And this was the perfect place for the proposal.

The garden was filled with autumnal colours: rust, emerald green and gold. Opa's vegetable patch, no longer tended to, had been overgrown with weeds, until Antje's husband had built a wooden gazebo over it where they sat together on wicker chairs and drank wine while their children played in the garden. I often wondered why Opa hadn't left the house to Mutti or Antje. Why me? Mutti had been resentful at first, but slowly accepted the fact that she was not suited to country living. Antje had shrugged off her hurt, pointing out that Opa had left her a tidy sum of money. But this "house of memories" was mine to keep or sell. I kept it.

Antje had strung up fairy lights in the gazebo, in anticipation of the proposal. There was a bottle of champagne chilling in the fridge too. My little sister had thought of every detail, beyond excited at the prospect of seeing me hitched.

I saw Klara hide a yawn behind her hand.

"Do you want to take a nap?"

She had been so sleepy the last few months. But she'd assured me that it was perfectly normal. During the first trimester, she'd said, the body was adjusting to the changes and using up all its energy.

"Yes, if you don't mind. I am still tired."

"No, of course not. Bedroom or sofa?"

"Sofa." She smiled at me gratefully as I covered her with Oma's crochet shawl. She was asleep within minutes.

I examined her face as she slept. There was a softness to her, an aura of innocence, which all the girls I'd dated had lacked. Maybe that's what drew me to her.

It was 3:30 p.m. Too early for a drink, so I thought to take a walk in the woods.

It had been many years since I'd walked here. The last time had been with Opa, who had stridden ahead, pointing out all the species of fern he could identify. Less than a month later, he would be dead.

"Keeled over in his garden patch..."

"Went quickly..."

"Didn't feel a thing..."

Words that washed over me, offering no succour at all.

I took a cigarette out of my pocket, lit it and placed it between my lips. Blowing out a smoke ring, I watched the water babble down the stream, and remembered.

"You cannot come back, Stefan!" She'd been emphatic, brooking no argument.

"Why not?" I'd looked at her wasted figure, her gaunt face, and felt unimaginably sad.

When she'd turned away from me, the bones in her upper back had jutted out painfully.

"Ingrid?" My voice was a whisper, a supplication.

"Marry your girl, have your baby. Don't come back here. It's for the best."

She'd closed the door on my face, turning me away once again.

"So you are marrying a woman you don't love?"

I turned slowly, deliberately. Heinrich was polishing his monocle on his waistcoat.

"I am."

"Because she's having your baby?"

"Because I'm tired, okay? I'm tired of chasing after a woman hell-bent on destroying herself. I'm tired of the games people play. I just want..." I stopped.

"What? What is it you want?"

"A bit of peace and quiet. A home, a wife, children."

"Is it fair to Klara?"

"I will be a good husband to her."

"And Ingrid?"

"There will be no more Ingrid."

Heinrich replaced his monocle and nodded.

"There are worse fates," he said before hopping away.

"You remember the first time I met you?"

I peered at him through an alcoholic haze. Heinrich looked exactly the same. It was I who had aged. At fifty, I looked ten years older and felt every one of my years. Today was my birthday, and I'd wandered into the woods to end it all.

It no longer surprised me to run into the *Osterhase*. He had welded himself so firmly into my life and my memories that I could not distinguish him from my own self.

"Yesssh," I slurred at him. "The globe..."

"I want to show you something. Come with me."

I stumbled after him. Minutes (or was it hours?) later, we stood near the stream. But this was somewhere I'd never been. This was a place where the stream bifurcated into two.

"I had wanted to show you then, but you were not willing. Perhaps now you will see?"

I watched the water catch the late evening light like jewels upon its surface. I watched it ripple over the rocks and pebbles, its colour changing from blue to grey to green. A tributary thinned out and flowed one way while the other flowed onwards through a thicket of trees.

Heinrich looked at me as though I needed to understand something important here. I didn't know what he wanted me to see. I shrugged my shoulders. So? A stream that went two ways. What was so interesting about that?

"Do you not see? Must I elaborate?" He asked me, his words sharp with impatience.

I stumbled away from him. I'd had enough of it all. No more riddles or puzzles, I was fed up to my back teeth.

"Stefan!" He called out, but I stumbled on blindly. Suddenly he was in front of me again, and in his pink eyes I saw something akin to pity. My face was wet with tears that I hadn't noticed I was shedding.

"Sit here for a while. Let's talk."

I shook my head. What was there to say?

"It needn't be this way," he said softly, "there is still much to be done."

"I... I cannot," I sobbed. "*Nein*[14]!"

"You must not give up."

"I cannot carry on."

I closed my eyes, and it felt as though everything was spinning out of control. When had it all gone so wrong? Was it when they had found Ingrid's body weeks after her overdose? Was it when Antje had finally succumbed to the cancer that had eaten her from the inside? Or was it when my alcoholism had cost me my job and my family?

I had nothing. I was nothing.

"But you see, that's where you are wrong. Look here." We stood in front of a shallow pond of water; algae crowding its surface, a rancid smell rising to meet our nostrils. Stagnant and still, the little tributary had emptied itself into this hollow where the water saturated the ground but moved nowhere. A breeding ground for mould, parasites and bacteria. The stench made me stagger back.

"This could be you..." Heinrich looked from the pool to me, then back again.

Suddenly we were in front of a large and brilliantly blue fresh-water lake; placid and glassy, serene and slow moving. The second tributary had emptied itself into its crystal depths.

"... or this could be you." Heinrich observed me as he said this, his pink eyes focussing on me intently.

I looked at the lake and shivered. It was astonishingly beautiful. Why had Opa and Oma never shown me this? It couldn't have been that far from the house, yet we'd never walked this way. Never even known of its existence.

What did Heinrich see in me that I didn't? How could he think I was still worth saving?

"Self-loathing serves nobody, least of all the one it inhabits."

"B... but, I have no one left... no one who loves me... or cares..."

"Is that really true, Stefan?"

My children's faces swam into view. Elsa, nearly fourteen, my *schatz*[15], daddy's girl; and Michael, my little boy who had cried as Klara had wrenched him out of my arms. My body heaved as I remembered all my past failures, and now, I'd been planning to fail them once again.

"Where do I go? What do I do?"

We were back in the woods, this time walking towards Opa's garden.

Heinrich walked up to the gazebo that Antje's husband had built all those years ago. The same gazebo where I had gone down on one knee in front of a pregnant Klara, the same gazebo where she had nursed Michael as I had played with Elsa, the same gazebo where Antje had kissed my cheek for the last time.

The years had taken a toll on the wooden frame; parts of it had rotted and buckled, parts had split, and in a corner there was mildew growing. I had not taken care of it, tended or maintained it. Life had removed the patina and replaced it with decay.

"Do you remember what lies beneath this?" Heinrich asked me.

"Yes, Opa's vegetable patch."

I remembered working with him, getting my hands dirty in the soil, feeling one with nature, that elusive feeling of pure contentment that I'd never experienced again.

"Maybe it's time to tear down the edifice and start from the ground up." Heinrich took off his monocle and rubbed it on the edge of his waistcoat.

"Maybe," I nodded, suddenly feeling clear-headed.

"Would you like to hand over that bottle of pills to me, then?"

Shamefaced, I took out the bottle and gave it to him.

"When will I see you again, *Osterhase*?"

Heinrich smiled a little sadly.

"Not for a while, Stefan. But I promise you, we will meet again."

Then, just as silently as he had appeared, he disappeared.

I sat waiting in the garden chair. It was nearly twilight, and even the birdsong had ebbed. There was a smell of smoke in the air, perhaps a garden fire somewhere.

"*Brauchen Sie irgendetwas*[16], Opa?" Antje, my granddaughter, fussed over me, her hands adjusting the blanket over my shoulders. I smiled up at her crookedly and shook my head to indicate that I didn't need anything. How much she looked like my little sister! When Michael had asked if he could name his daughter after Antje, I had choked up. Yet here she was, nine-years-old, the spitting image of my Antje.

"*Nein, schatz*[17]."

They had all come out to check on me one by one, surprised at my insistence on sitting out in the garden at dusk. It was cold and snow was forecast for the night. I shivered slightly, holding on to the warm mug of Ovaltine that Antje had brought out to me. Michael would have added a shot of brandy to it, just how I liked it.

The lights from inside cast a warm glow on the patio. I felt content, replete. The last thirty years had gone by in the blink of an eye. I was older than Opa had been when he died. Older than Mutti, Antje, Ingrid, and even Klara. I'd outlived them all. Yet, it felt as though they were around me, cocooning me with their love and guiding me with their wisdom, awaiting me with open arms.

The orphanage in Kathmandu still sent me weekly updates, pictures of the children they had taken in, the ones who'd made successful lives for themselves, and even the ones who hadn't. Elsa was there right now, overseeing the new wing they were constructing.

"They want to name it after you, Papa." She'd announced, her face flickering on the screen, her voice getting cut out. "You cannot keep denying them this. It was you, after all, who founded it. Let them repay you in this small way. It's not vanity, Papa, it's your legacy..."

The screen had gone blank before she could hear my response. Anyway, strong-headed as she was, I knew she would allow them to do it. It was my boy Michael who was the gentle and sensitive one. I saw so much of Antje in him, so much of me in Elsa. Who would guide them after I was gone?

I took the last sip of my Ovaltine before setting the mug down on the ground beside me. Heaving myself out of the chair, I hobbled over to the vegetable patch. Michael's wife, Marion, was a keen gardener, and she had expanded the patch, introducing newer vegetables, rotating the crop through the seasons. I thought back to Opa kneeling in the soil and smiled. He would have been pleased to see his patch flourish in this manner.

Leaning on my stick, I turned to look at the house. Oma and Opa had once resided there, then I had made it my home with Klara and the children, and now Michael and his family lived in it. Each generation had added its own stamp to it. But the beautiful, sprawling garden remained the same.

I doddered slowly to the edge of the garden and peered into the woods. The sun had set now, and the air was filled with the sweet noises of the small animals that lived there. Looking back at the house, I could make out the vague figures of Michael and his family, busy getting ready for dinner. Soon one of them would come outside to bring me in. I looked back at the woods and took a few faltering steps towards it. Somewhere within me there was a desire to see that cool, calm lake again. To revisit the moment that had changed the trajectory of my life over thirty years ago. But would this old and frail body make it there?

"Let me help you," Heinrich said softly at my shoulder.

"Ah, my old friend," I sighed, "I've missed you."

"Come." He led me through the woods, and it felt as though my entire body was weightless, moving rapidly through the trees—a chorus of browns and greens dimly lit by watery moonlight, the scent of a thousand living things mingling together, the joyful sound of the stream streaking through the terrain, carrying within it the secrets of all life.

Suddenly we stood on the banks of the lake, deep and still as it reflected the lunar crescent in the sky. Its inky blue was unfathomable, tranquil and accepting.

My eyes drank in the beauty of the landscape.

"It is time, is it not?" I asked the *Osterhase*, my friend and guide of a lifetime.

"Yes, Stefan, it is."

"Then I must return."

"I will take you."

"I have something of yours I need to give back." I held out the silver-rimmed monocle he had given me all those years ago. He accepted it, slipping it into his pocket. I hoped he would give it to someone else, someone who needed it just as much as I had.

"Thank you, Heinrich. For... everything."

He looked at me kindly.

"It has been an honour, my friend."

Then I was back in my chair. I looked around the garden once more, listened to the quiet babble of my family indoors, exhaled, then settled back and closed my eyes for the last time.

3
______

THE BUTTERFLY EFFECT

My *abuelo*[1] always said, "Whatever happens, happens for a reason." He'd never told me what his reason for moving from Buenos Aires to Puerto Iguazu was, but I suspected it was partly to do with my mother.

We ran a little B&B there called Hosteria Mariposa. It was sweet that he'd named it after me, but no one really called me Mariposa. I was always Mari - quiet Mari, poor Mari, orphan Mari. Hardly a 'butterfly', the stench of bad luck followed me as if it were oozing out of my very pores. Still, Abu always insisted that I was fortunate and as beautiful as a *mariposa*[2]. Of course he did! He was my grandfather, after all.

Our little hotel—and I called it a hotel, because I wanted it to be grander than it was, like the big American Hilton nearby—had only ten rooms. Each room, however, had its own distinct personality. This was more to do with the way that the property had been constructed rather than anything we'd done to it. Originally someone's home, rooms had been added over the years in an unusual and haphazard pattern, tacked on as an afterthought. Some rooms were long and rectangular, others were like little boxes, and one—the largest one—was like a pentagon. Guests were assigned rooms according to the rate they were willing to pay. And sometimes, Abu would give the pentagon room to a young, honeymooning couple who could barely afford it.

What I loved most about our hotel was its scent. The air was always heavy with the smell of dust and old wood. Rust and age filled the spaces, along with the aroma of something tangy and sweet. Then there was the sound of the Iguazu Falls crashing onto the rocks below. The rhythmic percussion of water echoed between the houses, bouncing from wall to wall; mingling with the creaking of the faucet and the squeaking of old doors. The wood on those doors and windows was rough and raw, filled with gnarly knots, and daylight streamed in through the cracks.

When Abu first bought the place, I was only five. But even then, he'd listened carefully to me as I ran through the rooms shouting, "Red!", "Blue!", "Pink!" The rooms were decorated accordingly and soon came to be known by their colours.

My favourite was the pentagon room, the "blue" of my childhood transformed into a turquoise wonder. The room was deep and oceanic; a king crab's shell, a palace of egg sacs and riches. The rug was locally sourced, a weave of sapphire, lime and maroon. An old and scarred oak table placed on one side of the room had been polished, and it reflected the light; a pale golden glow. A large bed covered in a mossy green coverlet took pride of place in the centre of the room, and an old dressing table with a mottled mirror reflected the azure richness of it all.

Every time I entered the room, I felt like I was plunging into the waters below the Devil's Throat, *La Garganta del Diablo*, and finding a place of sanctuary while the waterfalls cascaded, crashed and roared ferociously above me. In here, I was at peace.

It was also where Abu put me after the accident.

· · ·

I was only six months shy of turning eighteen when it happened. It was a beautiful day, and I was meant to help Abu with the hotel, but Diego was coming by on his new motorbike and I wanted to go with him.

"*Cariño*[3], he has just learned to ride. Maybe, it is not good to go out with him yet." My *abuelo*'s eyebrows knit together every time he worried, his craggy face creasing even more.

"Oh, Abu! Don't fret. I will be okay."

Young love and teenage impetuousness waved a red flag to fate that morning. When Diego's bike skidded at breakneck speed and landed heavily on its side, careening to a stop near a cliff edge, people said we were lucky. We could have gone over, we could have died. He suffered a concussion, but my left leg was crushed under the weight of the motorcycle, the bones splintering beyond repair. Yet, they said we were lucky.

The first thought I had in that moment was, can I survive this?

When I was four, my mother abandoned me. We were living in Buenos Aires at the time, in a small home in the San Telmo *barrio*[4]. My *abuela*[5] had died just a few months ago, and Abu was still recovering from losing his wife of over thirty years when Mama went out to a *milonga*[6] and never returned. Abu says she later sent word that she had met a man who wanted to take her travelling around the world. She said she would be back in a few months. Abu waited over a year, and when she did not return, he moved to Puerto Iguazu, his childhood home, and told everyone he knew to give Mama the address. She never came looking for us.

Mama was a tango dancer, like my *abuela* had been before her. But where it had only been a hobby for my grandmother, it was a passion for my mother. Abu would tell me she would practice for hours in front of the mirror, each move supple yet precise, each limb moving in time to the sharp, staccato rhythm of the *bandoneón*[7].

There were framed pictures of her all over the house. Dark hair pulled back into a small knot at the nape, her eyes large and luminous, her features delicate like her mother's had been. In every picture she was dancing, her body poised as if incapable of standing still; as if she wanted to slip away to a *milonga* immediately, leaving behind everyone and everything she knew.

I hated her, and I hated dance.

Abu often tried telling me stories of when she was younger, that stranger in the pictures. Of how funny and sweet she had been, how full of mischief, how loving. To me, she was only a woman in a picture frame. A woman that I bore a passing resemblance to but had little in common with.

You see, where my Mama was funny, I was serious; where she was sweet, I was acerbic; where she was loving, I was wary of love. Only Abu held my heart. Everyone else - Diego, and the boys that came before him, meant nothing to me.

"Tell me about my *Papi*[8], Abu..."

"What is there to tell, *princesa*[9]? Your mama was always an impulsive one. She only told us when she was five months gone, and I doubt that even she knew..."

When I looked in the mirror, I saw my mother's eyes, but the rest of me was someone I would never get to know. From my long limbs, to the cleft in my chin, and the way I devoured books, to my ability to swim like a fish; these were all genetic blessings from an unknown father. Yet, I felt closer to him than I ever had to my mother.

It was not like there weren't other maternal figures in my life. There was my teacher, *Seño* [10]Camila, who instigated my love of reading; our housekeeper, Maria, who bustled around our home as if it were her own, and was the closest thing to a mother I'd ever known. Also, I had many girlfriends who often tried practicing their motherly skills on me, perhaps in preparation for their future lives and children. I took what I needed from them and ignored the rest.

That is not to say that I was selfish! I was, and still am, a giver. I gave of my time and my patience. I also gave gifts to the people I was fond of. Jars of homemade *dulce de leche*[11], secondhand books, hand painted watercolours of the falls, pressed flowers that I turned into cards. These were all evidence of my affection. But I withheld a part of myself from everyone, a part I kept secure from hurt and betrayal. A part that was at the very core of who I was.

Maria often tried to get me to learn to dance.

"It is in your blood, Mari. Your *abuela* was a fantastic dancer."

Maria had known my grandparents when they were younger. They had all gone to school together and been friends for over fifty years. Now, Maria's daughter, Sofia, ran a dance school, teaching young children the basic moves of the tango: the rebounds, the quick side-steps, the stops on the beat.

"My blood is tainted by dance, Maria." I would answer flippantly, laughing as I gave my stock-standard response. "I would much rather read."

"And what will you do after all this reading?"

"Escape from Argentina and never come back!" I'd stick my tongue out at her then, and skip away, chuckling at her oaths.

The truth of the matter was that I did intend to leave. Perhaps Abu understood it, or at the very least, he suspected it. He was proud of my academic achievements, and happy to let me procure as many books as I liked from the secondhand store. Someday, I'd be a writer, but before that I planned to teach. I had already started looking into teaching Spanish as a foreign language, examining which certifications were recognised internationally, and how many countries I could travel to in the course of my career.

There would be days when I would chew on my lip in frustration, stomping around the kitchen while the old computer died and came back to life for the tenth time that day. Then I'd catch Abu's eye, as he watched me from his rocking chair, his bushy eyebrows forming a long horizontal band over his deep grey eyes. Then I would go and nuzzle into him, placing myself on his lap, breathing in his smoky cigar scent and allowing myself to be a five-year-old again.

On those days, he would pat my back and rock us both unevenly while whispering, "Don't run away from me yet, *cariño*." And we would both weep soft tears of grief and loss.

The long months of hospitalisation left me weak and my leg a useless, inky black log until finally it was amputated. The doctors in Puerto Iguazu said I could never use that leg again unless I was fitted with a prosthetic.

I remember little of that time, falling in and out of consciousness and pain. My dreams were dark and murky, hands reaching out from the mouth of *La Garganta del Diablo* and wrenching off my mermaid tail fin as I watched, helpless and incoherent in my anguish, knowing I would never swim again. The water from the falls crashed around me as I sank to the bottom, lifeless yet aware.

Mind flailing like jellyfish, lacking Lilliputian stability. The apparition of ghosts, the impairment of the future, a smell of death and decay mixed with the scent of moss and seaweed, a reeking marsh. And then, Abu leaning over me on my hospital bed, his face was so dear, his love like a salve to my soul, whispering, "Yesterday's pain is today's wisdom."

Was it all a dream?

I woke up in my blue pentagon room, a phantom itch on my absent leg driving me crazy. Reaching down, my hand met the nothingness of the amputation, and I screamed and screamed.

Abu's stocky figure rushed into the room, closely followed by Maria.

"Shhh, my *princesa*, my *preciosa*[12]! It is okay, it is okay."

He held me as I cried and beat his chest, and Maria uttered soothing words that did little to assuage the rage within me. Why hadn't I died? How could I live like this - a cripple! Where was the good Lord's justice?

I wish I could tell you that I healed quickly. Outwardly, I did, my young body recovering from the trauma of the accident and the amputation with remarkable resilience. But inside, I oscillated between rage and despair. And when I had no more tears and my throat was raw from screaming, I fell into a numb apathy. Refusing food, turning away from my books, ignoring the friends that came to visit. None of it mattered. My life was over.

Two months into my self-imposed exile, Abu came in and sat on the bed next to me.

"Mariposa, I want you to listen carefully to what I am going to say."

I was burrowed under the covers and gave no indication that I had heard, but something about his tone penetrated the fog of my gloom. That, and the fact that he rarely called me by my given name.

"Years ago, when you were only a little girl, a man came to stay here. He was a very handsome, distinguished-looking man, someone I would have put down to be a professor or in academia."

Reluctantly I turned towards him, shifting the coverlet off my face. Abu's face was grave, a faraway look in his eyes.

"I found it odd that this man would come here on his own. He seemed the sort who would travel in the company of a beautiful woman, or in a group of sophisticates. Why he would check into a humble B&B when he had access to a large and renowned hotel nearby also perplexed me. He handed me a large sum of cash as an advance to cover the cost of his stay. Naturally, I gave him this room."

I pushed myself up to recline against the headboard, interested now. Why hadn't Abu ever related this story to me before?

"Then?" I croaked, my voice an alien, unused entity.

"Something about the entire set-up bothered me all day. That night, on an impulse, I knocked on his door to offer him a glass of Malbec as a welcome drink. I knocked and I knocked, but he did not answer."

Abu sighed, resting his hands on his belly, remembering the events from that night long ago.

"I knew he hadn't left the hotel because I would have seen him leave. So, I entered the room with my spare key."

"What?" I gasped, knowing Abu never did that. He had drummed it into us as well. To never ever enter a room when a guest was in residence, and only to clean in their absence if they had instructed us to.

"Like I said, it was some sixth sense guiding me. I am glad I went in because I found him on the floor, a bottle of sleeping pills in his hand and a half empty bottle of whiskey on the table..."

I leaned forward, clutching at Abu's arm.

"Here? He died *here*?"

"When did I say he died? I took him to the hospital, where they pumped his stomach and kept him until he was fully recovered."

I fell back against my pillows in relief. Then I glared at Abu.

"Why did you tell me this story?"

"Because, *cariño*, he is coming here tomorrow, and he wants to meet you."

"Why?" I turned truculent immediately, angered by this imposition. Then, almost as an afterthought, I asked, "But why was he trying to kill himself?"

"Ah, that is not my story to tell. Maybe you can ask him yourself."

"I don't want to meet anyone!" I turned my face away.

"Mari, you will want to meet him." Abu put his hand under my chin, turning my face to him. "Remember when I said I'd thought he was a professor? I wasn't completely wrong. He was a doctor. And now, he has agreed to fit you for a prosthetic leg."

Rat-a-tat-tat, rat-a-tat-tat, rat-a-tat-tat.

I woke up to a strange noise coming from the corner of the room. Ever since I'd returned from Buenos Aires, sleep had become a complicated affair. It was as if my body had taken it upon itself to decide that all those months of depressed sleeping were quite enough, and now, my mind was always hyper-active and those same limbs that had been filled with lassitude itched to get up and move.

I sat up in my bed, back in my old bedroom, as the pentagon room was once again occupied by honeymooners. Turning on the bedside lamp, I peered into the corner where the odd noise had been emanating from. There was nothing there. Nothing except my prosthetic leg.

Looking at the leg brought all the memories of the past year flooding back. Dr Diaz's gentle hands, his encouragement, his understanding nature and, above all else, his generosity. Abu could never have afforded a state-of-the-art prosthetic limb on the *Obras Sociales*[13], but Dr Diaz had done it all for free through his foundation.

"Mari, your *abuelo* gave me back my life," he said when I queried him. "I'll never be able to repay that debt. This is only a tiny token of my gratitude."

Three months into the fittings and the physiotherapy, the daily evaluations and the psychological counselling, I finally gathered up the courage to ask him the question that had bothered me since the day Abu had told me his story.

"Why did you do it?" I blurted out in the middle of his note-taking, even as the nurse gave me a quizzical look. He'd motioned to the nurse to leave, and then turned towards me, his face serene.

"Are you asking me why I tried killing myself?"

I nodded, gulping, hoping I hadn't angered him.

He looked at his watch and then sat at the foot of my bed.

"Mari, you must know the feeling when you think that life isn't worth living anymore. I'm sure you have felt the same since the accident."

"Yes, yes, I did. But this," I looked down at the stump of a knee where my left leg used to be, "I hadn't expected to live like this."

He smiled then and patted the stump.

"You will do everything you've dreamed of, Mariposa. You will travel and you will teach; you will swim and you will dance. Nothing in your future will be impacted anymore."

"Not dance," I said, fervour making my words sharp.

"Very well. No dance." His eyes twinkled.

"But why did you feel that way? You look well. All your limbs are intact."

"Ah, but you see, I wasn't well. I was very, very broken on the inside."

"I don't understand?"

"Mari, do you know what HIV positive means?"

I nodded, my eyes widening.

"A friend, a dear friend, had just died from AIDS. And then I found out that I was HIV positive too." He shook his head lightly. "I thought it was better to end it then."

"But you are a doctor!"

"Yes, and clearly I was meant to live, and to keep practicing medicine. Thanks to your *abuelo*, I did. Then I realised how foolish I had been, and decided that the rest of my life would be spent helping people who had hit rock bottom - people like yourself."

"And your condition?"

"I have learned to live with it. As will you, no doubt."

Rat-a-tat-tat, rat-a-tat-tat, rat-a-tat-tat.

The noise had returned, and I could not understand where it was coming from. I grabbed the crutch that sat like a trusty old friend by my bedside, and hauled myself out of bed. Hobbling, I turned the main light on. Immediately my room was illuminated by the warm glow of the overhead bulbs. Unlike the pentagon room, my room was an amalgam of earthy browns, greens and rusts. An old, faded crocheted blanket, one that had belonged to my *abuela*, lay on my bed, and a framed print of two tango dancers sat just above my study desk. I would have gotten rid of it, except that all of *abuela*'s items were sacrosanct, and I didn't dare.

I moved towards the corner, flicking a glance at the clock on the wall. 3 a.m. What on earth was that noise?

As I approached the leg, I thought I noticed movement. Was the prosthetic moving on its own? But that was impossible!

I shivered as I recalled the feeling of wearing it and walking unaided for the first time. After months of visualising what my new leg would look like, I had been astounded to discover how very life-like it was. Then, when I had strapped it on and stood up, everyone in the room had applauded. Abu's face, his dear face, had been wet with tears.

Maybe that's why I hadn't mentioned the bolt of electricity that had shot through me, zinging every fibre of my being. I had felt über alive, as if the life energy of a hundred beings had gathered force within me. Then, as my audience waited for me to walk, I'd dismissed the feeling as nerves and proceeded to show them how well I was doing.

But every time I strapped the leg on, the feeling returned. And now this.

I reached forward and touched the leg that seemed to shiver in anticipation. My stump throbbed in response. It was as if they were communicating with each other. My body and this piece of foam-covered, carbon fibre and titanium limb!

Quite without knowing how, I strapped on the leg, as if in a trance. And that's when the trouble started.

The tango is, at its heart, a conversation. At first there is the *cabaceo*[14] —an invitation from the man to the woman—a nod after some eye contact, which is accepted or declined as per the woman's inclination. If accepted, the woman is led onto the floor and the discourse begins. The man leads, the woman follows, but not in the traditional way. She improvises, choosing how she wants to respond. Sensual and intimate, with a sense of longing permeating the movements and the music, there needs to be trust between the partners.

Closely attached at the chest or hip, they dance in unison to the rhythm, understanding instinctively where the other has come from and where they want to go. In the end, this cooperative process results in a highly improvisational dance, one that captivates the attention of both the dancers and the spectators.

· · ·

I was not a dancer, never had been nor intended to ever be. But my prosthetic leg had other ideas.

That night as I strapped it on in a daze, it started to move of its own volition, taking me through a complex series of steps made all the more difficult by the fact that I had no partner. My right leg followed obediently, and then my body had no choice. I spun and I whirled, I moved backwards and forwards, throwing my arms up, embracing an absent partner; my head held in the proud stance of a woman courted and admired by all. When the imaginary *bandoneón* music in my head came to its imaginary stop, my body halted, trembling.

The girl reflected in my floor-length mirror was one I didn't know. Wild-eyed, her hair in disarray and her pyjama top soaking with sweat, she looked alive. More alive than she had in months.

I collapsed onto my bed, stunned. What had just happened? Looking down at the prosthetic attached to my knee, I shuddered. Unsnapping it violently, I threw it across the room. Then I turned my back to it and sobbed into my pillow. Was I losing my mind now?

The next morning, I hobbled into the kitchen using my crutch. Abu looked up from doing his accounts and started.

"*Cariño*, are you in pain? Is the leg uncomfortable?"

"No, no. I… just wanted a break from it, that's all."

Maria handed me a *café con leche*[15] and laid a plate of *medialunas*[16] on the table, her eyebrow raised in disbelief.

Abu carried on. "You do not have to worry about wearing it out, Mari. Dr Diaz has promised that all future replacements will be taken care of by the foundation."

I sipped at my coffee, not meeting their eyes. How could I explain that the leg scared me? How could I explain that I feared the person I became when I wore it? They would think me mad. I half-thought I was losing my mind.

"Eat! You are too thin, Mari," Maria scolded me. "Diego wants to come by today. He asked me yesterday if it was alright. I said okay."

"Why? If it wasn't for that *forro*[17], Mari would be whole!" Abu roared.

But Maria stood her ground.

"Our Mariposa is whole - with or without her leg! Diego has been trying to come and apologise for the past year, and you have not allowed him to. I think it is time."

I watched as they both stared at each other intensely before Abu lowered his gaze. Maria had won this round.

Upstairs I strapped on the leg, hoping it wouldn't do anything foolish, but it was as docile as a lamb. I put on the emerald green dress that hugged me in all the right places, and pinched my cheeks to inject some colour in them.

Truth be told, I was nervous about seeing Diego after all this time. When I had flirted with him before, it had been with impunity, secure as I was in my skin; in my ability to detach myself whenever I chose. Now, I was a different person. Damaged, incomplete, incapable. How would he view me?

Diego was a catch, all my girlfriends used to tell me. Tall, curly-haired, dimpled, clever and with a smile that could melt the hardest of hearts, he also had a bit of the daredevil in him. Maybe that was what attracted me to him. In the year gone by, when my entire world had tilted off its axis, Diego had fallen off it too.

Now, as I made my way downstairs, my heart hammered in my chest. What would he say? What would I say in return?

He stood by the stove, his entire posture one of abasement. It was no wonder as my *abuelo* was staring daggers at him. If not for Maria, who stood between them, arms crossed, there might have been a bloodbath in our kitchen.

As I stepped into the room, a sudden ray of light caught me mid-step, blinding me for just a moment. I heard a collective gasp and as I stepped out of it, I looked at Abu's face, which had turned ashen.

"Abu, what is it? Are you okay?"

Before I could reach him, Diego caught him as his knees buckled.

"W... what happened?" I rushed over, my gait slightly awkward.

Maria laid a hand on my shoulder. "For a minute there, Mari, you looked exactly like your mother."

"Oh."

I looked from her face to Abu's and noted the shock written on them.

"I'm sorry," I muttered.

"Ah, don't be silly, *niña*[18]. It has nothing to do with you. Go out now. I will tend to your *abuelo*. Diego, you take her outside now, *che*[19]!"

In the small garden outside our part of the B&B, we had wicker furniture with bright orange cushions, which were always piled up in a corner to protect them from the rain. Diego put them down on the chairs, and we both sat across from each other.

"Mari," he started, his voice hoarse.

"Diego," I jumped in, "please don't. There's no need. It was an accident and I am not angry with you. I don't hold you responsible."

He held my gaze for a moment before dropping his face into his hands. His shoulders shook as he cried quietly, the occasional sniff escaping him. Appalled, I moved my chair closer to him, reaching one hand out tentatively to pat his arm.

He held on to my hand, raising his tear-streaked face to stare at me.

"I haven't slept well in over a year. Mari, I keep replaying that day in my mind. What if I had gone slower, what if I hadn't skidded, what if it was I who had lost my leg?"

"So many what-ifs, Diego," I sighed. "What difference does it make? What's done is done."

"But..."

"Shhh." I placed my finger on his lips. "I cannot live with regret any longer, and I don't want you to either."

Clasping both my hands, he leaned forward and kissed me softly. He tasted of salt and coffee, and in spite of myself, I melted into him. The soft kisses turned more passionate as he wound his fingers through my hair, pulling me closer. I allowed myself to drown in his ardour for a few more minutes, before pushing him away and standing up.

"I don't want your pity, Diego."

"Pity? Is that what you think this is?"

He stood up behind me, put his hands on my shoulders, and turned me around to face him.

"Even you must know, Mari, that I have been in love with you since I was ten. When you finally agreed to go out with me, I was *extático*[20]! Then I messed it all up."

I stared at him.

"You don't want me now, Diego. This is just guilt talking. I am not the same girl you took to the *cine* [21]or to drink *mate*[22] with friends. I have changed, and not just physically."

"But my feelings for you have not changed! When your *abuelo* would not allow me to see you, and when you went to Buenos Aires for your operation, I went mad with worry! I hounded Maria night and day to intervene on my behalf. Mari, believe me when I say that I would marry you tomorrow, if I could!"

I looked at the handsome boy in front of me and wondered what to say. So much was unresolved within my own self that I could not take on the weight of someone else's feelings, too.

"Diego, please don't be offended, but I cannot do this right now."

His face fell as he regarded me.

"You do not love me."

I turned away from him.

"I don't know what I feel anymore. Please, just give me time."

He dropped a soft kiss on my head and left.

.   .   .

"Well?" Maria asked as soon as I went indoors.

"Nothing. He asked for forgiveness and I forgave him."

Abu grunted from his rocking chair.

"As if that will bring your leg back."

And just as soon as he'd said that, my left leg seemed to wake up. Diego, who I thought had left, returned with a book in his hand, a book I had lent him a long time ago.

"I forgot... I meant to give this back..."

But his words were lost in the flurry of what occurred then.

Tipping forward, I grabbed his body, and suddenly and sensuously, my hip attached itself to his. Diego, who had been dancing at *milongas* for as far back as he could remember, responded intuitively to my unspoken invitation.

We moved together in the 8-count basic. Diego settled on his right leg, placing me on my left. Then he stepped side left, and I, side right. He turned forward right in the outside right position, keeping his upper body turned towards me, while I paralleled him in contrabody. He stepped forward left, and I stretched back right, seeking his centre. He closed his right foot to his left and rotated his upper body to face forward, while I crossed my left foot in front of the right as I finished moving back in front of him. We went from the *salida* [23] to the *resolución* [24] within minutes. Then, just as abruptly as it had begun, it stopped.

I stepped away from him, my face flooding with embarrassment. He goggled at me, as if I had grown two heads. Had I? Nothing was impossible now!

"But you said you hated the tango!" He blurted out, his eyes still bulging. I thought back to all the times I'd rejected his invitations to the *milongas* he frequented.

I shook my head reflexively, then looked at Abu who sat open-mouthed in his rocking chair, having forgotten to rock.

Then Maria stepped forward and handed me a glass of water.

"When did you learn, Mari?"

That was when my body decided that the best course of action would be to faint.

. . .

"You say it's the leg?" Maria's incredulity wasn't entirely unwarranted.

After I had been revived, I found myself on the sofa sipping on a *submarino*[25]. Maria's version of it was especially delicious because she melted an entire bar of El Alguila chocolate into warm milk and then topped it with a sprinkling of cinnamon, adding her signature dash to it. The *submarino* was reserved for special occasions, and fainting spells now, I guessed.

Abu and Diego sat together, for once not in disagreement with each other. They were both looking at me with an expression of stunned wonderment.

"I can't explain it," I shrugged, "it decides when and where it wants to dance, and then the rest of my body just obeys."

I looked at the offender which sat mute and innocent, still attached to my knee, but no longer trembling to dance.

"But how is that possible, *cariño*? Dr Diaz does not manufacture magical limbs." Abu finally spoke, his voice shaking.

"And the way you moved... it was like a professional." Diego's voice was accusing.

"Like I said," I shouted, "I don't know how or why this is happening! I can't explain it and it's driving me *loca*[26]!"

"*Cálmate*[27], Mari! We are all just shocked, that is all." Maria sat down heavily in the armchair. "Do you think we should contact this Dr Diaz?"

"And say what? That the leg is defective because it makes me dance? He will laugh at us."

"Juan Diaz is not the sort of man to laugh at anyone, but he has done us enough favours without us bothering him with something like this too." Abu stroked his chin. "Anyway, Mari, what harm is there to it? You didn't dance before, and now you do. Another talent to add to all the rest."

"You must be joking, Abu! The one thing I hate is the very thing this leg is making me do. Besides, there is no controlling it. It starts up anywhere, anytime. Can you imagine how embarrassing that is for me?"

"You were embarrassed to dance with me?" Diego sounded hurt.

"Of course not! That is not what I am saying. But what if tomorrow it isn't you? What if it is Pedro, the postman? Or, Mateo, the delivery boy?"

All of us sat in silence. Then Maria spoke up.

"Only one solution I can think of. You learn to control it, instead of it controlling you."

"How?"

"Let me ask Sofia if she will give you private lessons. She is my daughter, she will listen to me."

I groaned out loud.

"One more person who will think that I have gone mad!"

"No one thinks that, *princesa*!" Abu glared at Diego as he said this.

"I can take you!" Diego offered with an apologetic glance at Abu.

"On your motorcycle...?" Abu growled.

"No, no! I got rid of it. Now, I have a small Fiat Focus, and," he raised his hands as if to ward off any objections, "I will drive slowly and carefully. Please let me do this for Mariposa."

Once again, we sat in silence, not sure what the future held for us, but convinced that in my case, it would take far more than two to tango!

"Does it hurt when you tango?" Sofia asked, visibly perplexed.

"Not at all! It twinges occasionally when I walk or put extra pressure on it, but when I dance, it moves as freely as my right leg. Even more, actually."

"Hmmm. Well, it seems to me that you know the basic steps. What you need to learn is control. So," Sofia stood up and walked to the end of the studio and turned the music on. Strains of Anibal Troilo's *"Quejas De Bandoneón"* flooded the room.

"Come, let us practise."

Diego watched from one end of the studio as I held Sofia's hand

and stood up. My right foot tapped to the music, but the left refused to cooperate.

"It doesn't want to," I muttered dolefully.

"Make it." Sofia countered.

"How?"

"Close your eyes. Listen to the music. Let it enter your mind and body, let it penetrate your soul."

Grumpily, I obeyed.

Slowly, I got caught up in the sway and sweep of the rhythm - happy one minute, plaintive the next; joyous and romantic, recalling lush moments in the sun, moments of love, of kissing underwater, of swimming naked in the moonlight - and suddenly, my leg came alive. My eyes snapped open, and instead of Sofia, it was Diego standing in front of me.

He held out his hand, and I took it.

Once again I was transported, led into the intimacy of dance, unwittingly. But this time, halfway through, Sofia stopped us. Diego complied, holding me in a clasp that made movement impossible. My left foot still tapped impotently, but the rest of my body was static.

The music carried on. I closed my eyes and tried communicating with my prosthetic leg. "It's okay", I whispered under my breath, "the music will still be there. You and I can dance to it another time." Immediately, my foot stopped tapping.

"Did you do that?" Sofia asked.

"Yes, but I'm not sure I can control it completely."

"It will take time. Keep coming to the lessons. Maybe you can even go to a few *milongas* with Diego."

I shuddered at the thought, but almost straight away, my left foot responded by tapping in rhythm to the *bandoneón* strains.

"Okay, okay, I'll go." I glared at the leg and then at Sofia and Diego in turn.

"Sometimes Mariposa, we just have to go with the flow." Sofia nodded sagely.

~

In the months that followed, if I wasn't reading, I was dancing. People commented on how light on my feet and lithe I was. For those who didn't know or didn't look too closely, it seemed as if I was complete, with all my limbs intact. My dancing had also progressed from the tango *basico* to the more advanced *volcadas, calesitas, planeos* and *barridas*.[28]

"She is Elena's granddaughter..."

"Ah, but she is Lucia's daughter..."

Everywhere I turned I heard my *abuela*'s name, which made me happy, or my mother's, which angered me.

"There is no escaping your bloodline, *cariño*." Abu, calm and fatalistic, who had accepted every peak and trough of his life, exhorted me to accept this twist of fate in mine.

When I hadn't been to see *Seño* Camila in three months, she came to see me.

Slim and bespectacled, she had been the benefactor of many books and was concerned that I hadn't been to return the last loan.

"I still have them *Seño*, I just haven't finished them yet."

"That is unusual for you, Mari. Normally, you read them thrice in half the time. Is it true what I hear about you?"

She studied me from behind the glasses as my head dipped in confusion.

"Are you dancing at *milongas* now? Some say that you plan to compete professionally? Have you decided against teaching then?"

"I... I don't know..." I stammered in confusion. And honestly, I didn't.

But her words reminded me of my first love, and once again, I returned to the world of words and stories, forsaking the tango as long as my now semi-controlled prosthetic leg allowed me to.

Diego had become as attached to me as the prosthetic. He had won over my *abuelo* with his dedication, and Maria, always trembling at romantic *telenovelas*[29], was encouraging him openly. It was I who was resistant.

"Mari, why won't you believe me when I say I love you?"

"Because, Diego, love means nothing. For now, you claim to love me. Tomorrow, a more beautiful girl crosses your path, and you may fall in love with her. What happens then?"

"Why are you so cynical?"

"I am pragmatic and so should you be. All this dancing around me has to stop. What of your Dentistry?"

Diego had been accepted into the University of Salvador, but had delayed his start by a year. He wouldn't say why, but I suspected it was because he wanted to move there the following year when I went to study at Universidad de Buenos Aires.

"There are things I need to settle before I go." He looked away as he said this, which only reinforced my belief. "Anyway, will you come to the *milonga* this Saturday?"

Lately I'd been skipping them, able to control the prosthetic better, promising it another evening, another time.

"I have to study for my exams, Diego. You know that."

"It is the last one I will ask you to, then you can knuckle down to your studies."

The foot had started its tap-tapping once again.

"There she goes, little *Maricita*[30]!" Diego remarked fondly. He had developed an affection for my prosthetic leg, and exasperated as I was by his attachment to me, I couldn't help smiling in return.

"Oh, very well! Pick me up at 11 then."

My last *milonga* was once again in a disused warehouse that was often utilised as a place for these tango dance-events. Once nearly demolished, it was rescued by an anonymous patron and given over to the organisers of *milongas*.

Inside, the lights were dim, and the *milongueros*[31] were gathered, awaiting their turn on the floor. With the first *cabaceo*, a couple moved to the centre of the floor. The woman was dressed in a shocking pink dress with a fringed hem. Her dark hair was pulled back into a low chignon and she wore a beautiful bronze hair clip on the right side of her head. The man was older, grey-haired, with a long moustache and a low, thin ponytail. Dressed in a white silk shirt and dark trousers, he moved with the effortless grace of a panther.

"Who are those two?" I whispered to Diego.

He shrugged, his eyes not moving from them. He was not alone. All eyes were on the couple that danced with a rich, sensual ease. Their comfort with each other was apparent to all, but their dance was almost shockingly erotic. A languid slink that morphed into a rapid swirl, it stirred up forbidden desires in all the onlookers. With every backward kick, every sudden dip, they held the audience in their thrall. Their dance was like a complete love affair—erotic and charged—with not one word exchanged.

No one else dared to step onto the floor whilst the two danced with such grandeur and sensuality that everything else paled in comparison.

When they finally finished and took their bows, the room exploded in applause. For the first time, I felt moved to tears. This was true tango - in all its beauty, melancholy and nostalgia. This was worth living or dying for.

Slowly the dance floor filled up again, and Diego led me with a quick, "Come".

I felt inadequate, stumbling over my feet, feeling the weight of my prosthesis.

"What is it, Mari?"

"I can't dance."

"But of course you can."

"No, I think it's gone, Diego. I'm not feeling it anymore."

He led me off the floor to a quiet corner.

"Are you okay?"

Stricken, I shook my head. How quickly I had become accustomed to how the tango made me feel. How good it was for my body; how much I used it, like meditation or therapy. And now that it had forsaken me, I was devastated.

"I think I'd like to go home."

He drove me home wordlessly, planting a quick kiss on my hand before I exited the car.

"I'll call tomorrow."

I nodded, tears slipping down my face noiselessly.

In my room, I took off the prosthetic leg and placed it to a side.

"Where did you go, my little djinn of dance?"

The leg remained motionless, a mute piece of foam-covered carbon fibre and titanium limb.

After a sleepless few hours, I finally fell into a deep, dreamless slumber just as the first rays of sunshine poked their way in through the cracks in my shutters. I slept soundly until noon and woke up with my heart hammering against my ribcage. Why had no one woken me? Where was Maria, who normally bustled in at 8 a.m. regardless of how late a night I might have had?

I grabbed my crutch, ignoring the prosthetic, and hobbled my way into the kitchen.

There was a strange charge in there, as if all the electrons had rearranged themselves and created a different energy. Maria was busy at the stove and as I walked in, she looked up at me, her expression unreadable. Her eyes were red, as if she had been crying.

"Abu?" The question came out as a plea, my heart constricting at the thought.

"No," she mouthed quietly, tilting her head towards the living room. I stumbled my way towards the living area, wondering what awaited me.

Inside, there were the signs of a most civilised lunch. *Empanadas*[32] and *fainâs*[33], *chimichurri* [34]and *provoleta*[35] jostled for space with *alfa-jores*[36] on our narrow coffee table. Most of it remained uneaten. Two visitors sat across from my *abuelo*, talking in low tones. They stopped as soon as I walked in.

Startled to recognise them as the couple from last night, I came to a halt as well.

That's when the woman, dressed elegantly in a cream shirt and slacks, came towards me, a timid smile on her face.

"Mariposa, it is I, your mama."

I took a step back, stumbling at first, then regaining my balance. Then I turned my back on her and limped my way back to my room, closing the door with a loud thud and locking it behind me.

For the next few hours I did not respond to Abu's entreaties or Maria's appeals. Not until I was sure that the visitors had left did I emerge from my room.

Diego was sitting with Abu, looking worried, as Abu spoke softly to him. Maria was nowhere to be seen.

"Why," I asked, ferocious in my anger, "why did you let her in?"

Abu held out his arms, and instinctively I hobbled over and buried myself in his chest, sobs racking my body.

"She is your mama, Mari."

"She is nothing to me. You are my mama and my *papi*."

"But Mariposa, don't you want to know what happened to her?"

"No!" Stubborn, I held on to my only anchor, rigid in my hatred for the woman who had birthed me.

If life was like a book, then there would be answers to all the questions. But life is always stranger than anything fiction could conjure up. When Lucia had left home on a whim, tempted by a handsome man's offer, she had not expected to be sold into slavery. Taken to Saudi Arabia, held against her will and living a life of domestic servitude, it was only years of patience, and one tiny window of chance that had led to her escape.

She sat in front of me, this beautiful stranger that I had hated for nearly all my life, and wept openly. Tears of remorse, tears of guilt, and tears of redemption.

"My darling girl, my darling Mariposa! The only thing that kept me going was the thought of you. The thought that someday I would get to see you, to hold you."

Lucia reached forward, but I shrank from her touch still. I was ready to listen, but I wasn't yet ready to forgive.

"I was impetuous and foolish," she acknowledged, "but I more than paid for my sins. If only you knew of the life I led..." Her last words caught on a sob.

"But you are still dancing. I saw you at the *milonga* that night."

"Yes," she nodded, brightening slightly, "It was dance that took me away from you, and it is dance that has brought me back."

She looked at the man sitting next to her, her love for him apparent in the gaze she threw him.

"If it weren't for Carlos, I may not have survived. When I ran away from my employers while they holidayed in London, I was penniless; without a passport or any kind of identification, and unable to speak a word of English. Carlos found me on the streets, wandering like a street urchin, begging for food."

"How fortunate that he also happened to dance the tango!" Disbelief dripped from my words.

Lucia folded her delicate hands on her lap and looked at me.

"I believe you also dance the tango, and with no formal training either?"

All my words choked up as I realised that I alone did not reserve the right to remarkable events or coincidences.

I nodded, my eyes meeting hers in a sudden recognition of life's randomness and chaos, of its incredible vagaries and miracles.

"Show me," she implored.

"I... I don't know if I can..."

"Try," she whispered.

I stood up, just as she did. Her eyes locked with mine, followed by a tilt of her head, and I acknowledged her *cabaceo*. With a swift move, she suddenly held me in her arms. The melody of a thousand *bandoneóns* erupted somewhere, and my left foot started its familiar tap-tapping.

As we bent and swirled, moved forwards and backwards—my mama and I, in a dance as old as Argentina itself—I felt all the missing parts of me fall into place.

And I was complete once more.

4

———

NEW YEAR, NEW YOU

I died here, or perhaps you could say that I was born here. But I shall come to that in a moment.

First, I want to ask you - how is your New Year working out? How are the resolutions, the vows of change, the promises you make to yourself annually working for you?

I'm always amazed by the human capacity for self-delusion and optimism. You would think that after years of failing, humankind would have given up on the very idea of changing themselves, of making promises they cannot keep. But no, the charade carries on year after year. And I watch, amused in the knowledge that most of you will not succeed in your endeavours.

Who am I, you ask? That is a fair question.

I am not God, if that's where your line of thought was taking you. But I am not the Devil either. I walk amongst you, I reside within you, and every seventy years or so, I look for a new host. Creeps you out a bit, doesn't it? But you started this, so don't complain now.

I was perfectly happy where I was, doing the job I was meant to: guarding my master for all eternity. Then you came along with your pickaxes, your drills, your thirst for knowledge. Little did you know that your curiosity would unearth far more than you'd bargained for. But once again, I race ahead of myself.

What I really want to ask you is this: have you learned anything at all from history? If not, and in my eyes, clearly not, then why disturb those who want to lie in peace? If it is to indulge your childish curiosity, then be prepared for the consequences too.

You look at me now, all wide-eyed in your innocence and naïveté. You asked to be here; you asked to interview me, so you must have known a bit about me before you came here. Why pretend then? Ah, I see your mask drop a little. You do know, and you're afraid. That is wise, little one. Be afraid, be very, very afraid. But first, have a drink. There is an excellent claret in that drinks' cabinet over there. Pour me one too. I may look like an old man, but certain appetites remain as voracious as always.

Come and sit across from me again. There is no point in trying to adjust the shawl, let it just stay on my knees. This body is beyond any help now, and before long, will be consigned to a grave. I, of course, will move on. That is what I do.

Where to? Oh, aren't you a nosy one! Let's take this one step at a time, shall we? Where do I begin... Hmmm, let's see... Isn't there a song that goes—let's start at the very beginning? Well, let's start there then.

I was born in Egypt many, many years ago. Much before all the Gods you worship now even existed. From the very beginning, I was indentured to the service of my king, all but a boy himself. You know his name, so I will not mention it. But hear this - even if I could, I would not let his name cross my lips. It is the gravest disrespect to talk of my master in this manner.

After all these years, you ask? Always, is my answer. My loyalty and love for my master started this chain of events. Now, I enjoy it for what it is, but back then, I was acting out of anger and a desire for justice.

Your historians have never found out how he died so young, nor will they ever. I know, but will I tell? Ah! Look at you now, leaning forward in curiosity. You are desperate to know. But if I tell you, I'll have to kill you. I am serious.

Ha! Ha! Ha!

You recoil so spectacularly! Shall we leave it then, this topic of his death, and move on to the topic of mine? Suffice it to say that his was not a natural death. All those rumours... I won't tell you which one is true, but he did not die of natural causes. I, on the other hand, chose to accompany him. My weapon of choice was a dagger. Right here, to my heart. This was my fealty to my king, my duty to my lord.

They buried him with all the pomp and splendour that was his due. All his organs were removed and placed in special containers. Each jar had the head of a God carved on it to protect its contents, but my master's heart remained within his body. After all, that would be weighed in his afterlife to judge how good a life he had led.

My king's body was preserved, then wrapped up in linen and placed in a gold coffin. A beautiful gold death mask adorned it, mirroring his boyish good looks. Amulets and jewels were buried with him, and food, water and wine placed in the chamber to accompany him on his journey to the afterlife.

You seem bored, almost. Of course, you know all of this, you've studied it for many years. But you cannot imagine the pleasure it gives me to remember. So, you must bear with me even if it means sitting through an extra ten minutes of my rambling. Indulge an old man, will you?

Where was I? Ah, yes.

The walls of his tomb were covered with beautiful paintings that told stories of how he would travel from the burial procession to the passage through the Underworld and into the afterlife. He had several changes of garments, tunics, scarves and headdresses to help him look his best when he arrived. There were games to keep him busy, perfumes to keep him fragranced, weapons to protect him, spells from the Book of the Dead to help him pass into the afterlife, and chariots to help him navigate the difficult terrain.

And then there was me.

A mere boy myself, I was buried at his feet in an unmarked grave. I had just one duty. To protect him in death, as I had in life.

Only, I had failed at this duty, hadn't I? I could not protect his life. It was snatched in the most brutal manner, and I was a mute spectator, helpless and terrified. Before plunging the dagger into my heart, I had sworn that I would not fail him in the afterlife. My wish to be buried with my master had been vouchsafed by the royal household itself.

For many years we lay together in peace. I had seen him off on his journey, promising to always stand guard at the foot of his coffin, and I was as good as my word.

What of my own afterlife, you ask? What of it? Do you think I was entitled to anything after my betrayal? Thousands of years of penitence is what it takes to wipe out one instance of treachery.

How your eyebrows rise to your hairline! Aha, now you think you understand, but do you really?

The light is fading outside. Perhaps it's time to turn on the lamps. Would you mind?

Thank you.

Have you looked outside yet? No? Step out onto the balcony and gaze upon that view. Look how gently the Nile flows, watch how the dying rays of the sun dance upon the pyramids in the distance. Tranquillity and beauty, I am surrounded by it all. It's ironic how I always return to my birthplace to die.

I've come here in various incarnations - as a proud aristocrat, a humble wayfarer, an explorer, a mendicant, a seer, a sage, a warlock, a woman, an academic and too many other guises to mention. Life after life, I return hoping that one day I will receive my longed-for absolution. But, until that happens, I might as well enjoy the journey.

You can come back in now. Draw those muslin curtains, will you? I like to gaze upon the lights of the marina.

Are you enjoying the claret? You haven't drunk much of it. I acquired a taste for it... oh, about three hundred years ago. I drink nothing else now. It rather suits all the bodies I inhabit. Look at this one, for instance. Nearly a hundred years old! A good claret can keep a bad body going for a lot longer than expected.

That's it, drink up. Cheers!

Now, where was I?

Treachery, yes.

Indentured as I was, I wasn't resentful. My family had been enslaved for two generations before me and had risen in the ranks to serve the royal household, eventually.

Grandfather had told me stories of a life before, in a land far, far away. But he'd only been a boy himself when he was captured in the war and brought back as a prisoner. He had been smart enough to adapt to his new surroundings quickly, sharp enough to learn and grow, and eventually inveigle his way into the affections of a nobleman. From then onwards, he had risen steadily, ensuring a secure future for himself and his progeny. It was at his behest that I was presented to the boy pharaoh as a playmate, companion and guard.

The honour of tasting his food and sipping his wine was mine; that of waking him every morning too. We played together, we ate together, we laughed together. We were brothers in every way but by name.

What was that you said? Say it again. My hearing is not very good.

Ahh! You are in a hurry and want to get to the heart of the matter. Why? Will you produce a paper saying you know the cause of his mysterious death? Who will believe the ramblings of an old man? What proof would you have, anyway?

Oh, I see. This is to satisfy your own curiosity, is it? "Area of expertise" and all that. Tell me, how did you find your way to me? I've covered my tracks very well, except for that one time... But we don't need to speak of that. A happy accident, you say. Well, I will be the judge of that.

How's that claret doing? Go on, pour yourself some more and top mine up too. There are some dates there, by the sideboard. Try one. They're absolutely delicious with this. I see from your expression that you are not fond of dates. That is a shame, as they are of excellent quality. Never mind, I shall enjoy them on my own.

My liege lord was insanely fond of dates. If he could have, all he would have consumed would have been dates and milk. Often I would give him my share too, to indulge his sweet tooth.

So, as you can tell, we were more friends than master and slave. But just as every master has his secrets, every slave has his too.

My reports on the young pharaoh went directly to my grandfather who then fed them to the boy king's enemies. And there were plenty of those. Although he was a direct descendant of the pure line of ruling pharaohs, there were many who wished to depose him. His father's policies had been unpopular; angering the priesthood, cutting loose many allies and endangering the future of our nation by forcibly quelling dissent. The boy king did not know any better, so continued in the same vein as his father, despite his many advisors counselling him to use softer tactics. But his loyalty to his father was legendary. Sadly, it would also lead to his downfall.

What is that smell, you ask. That is *feseekh* - mullet fish caught in the Mediterranean and stored within wooden barrels. Its innards are left intact, and it's packed in salt for forty-five days. Yes, it stinks, but it is a delicacy. Egyptians enjoy it during the festival of *Sham el-Nessim*, which we've been celebrating since the age of the pharaohs. My local fishmonger considers himself quite the expert in it, and every so often you will get a whiff in the air. A garbage dump, you say? No, no, do not insult an Egyptian in this manner. It's very fetidness is its distinction. You must try it before you leave Cairo, but be warned: inexpertly done, it can lead to paralysis and even death.

So, as I was saying, the young pharaoh's policies were just as inflexible as his father's. Perhaps to divert his attentions, he was advised to marry. He was twelve years old, and his marriage was arranged to his cousin who was fifteen. Now, this was unusual even for its time. Not because of the incestuous nature of the relationship, but because of the age of the principles. You see, at fifteen, the future queen had already been married and widowed once. Normally a pharaoh would marry at eighteen, and if not a princess to strengthen a political alliance, then a young girl on the cusp of puberty. But my lord had set his eyes on his cousin only once and had been smitten ever since. Even I had to admit privately that she was quite a delicious creature, although my tastes did not run in that direction. Full-chested, with a tiny waist and ample hips, she was every young boy's dream. Also, having birthed two infants already, her fertility was not in question either.

For two years after their wedding, my young lord was distracted enough not to question the re-emerging power of the priesthood or the reports of uprisings on his borders. A nubile woman can be a most attractive diversion. But when the queen fell pregnant for the third time, and the pharaoh had exhausted his appetites on the slave girls, his mind was once again focussed on the politics of his land.

At fourteen, he had already filled out and cut an imposing figure. When he saw all the changes that had taken place beneath his nose, his anger knew no bounds! Six priests were put to death before my very own eyes. A hush-hush war plan was drawn up to quell the uprisings, only his inner circle privy to his plans.

Of course, I was funnelling all the information to my grandfather, who was using it for means fair or foul; I did not know which. It ensured our family's fortunes, and as heir to those, it was my duty to perform the task set for me.

Here, I hasten to add: I was neither gullible nor conniving. I was, perhaps, a bit too trusting. In my mind, I was fulfilling my duty to my family and to my king as well. In no way did I ever envision that the two might have been at odds with each other.

What's that? As I said before, you need to speak up!

Oh, my language... Ha! Ha! Ha! You call it old-fashioned. My dear boy, I have had to adapt to so many languages and dialects that you cannot even imagine. But like my grandfather, I have always been a quick learner. I do retain traces of ummm... formality in my tongue. But you will find that I can speak the slang of any youth in any land just as well. Your Charles Darwin talked about how species that adapt well to their environment have the best chance of survival. Well, guess what I've been doing for thousands of years?

What time is it? Nearly 7 p.m. you say. Goodness! Perhaps you'd like to join me for dinner? No, no, it is not an imposition at all. I like to eat early. This body does not digest food after 8 p.m.

You will have to help me with heating things up. The cook has left a meal in the refrigerator for me. I assure you there will be enough. Yes, right through there. I will follow you, but slowly. It takes an age to get this body moving, it's no longer as sprightly as it once was; as you yourself are now.

Let us see what we have here - *kushari*[1], *kofta*[2] and *ful medames*[3]. Perfect! A typical Egyptian meal for us to share. You are a meat-eater, aren't you? Good, good. How is that claret doing? Nearly at the end of the bottle, are we? Then perhaps we should open another one. Wine makes me garrulous. Surely the result you want?

Come, come, don't be shy now. You are here, enjoy the company of this old man and bear with his ramblings. What treasure you may walk away with, think of that!

Here, place the food on this table, right here. There are plates inside that sideboard. Perhaps you would be kind enough to place them on the table too?

How do I manage here on my own?

Well, the cook comes every day and prepares my food. The cleaner comes daily as well. As for the rest of the time, I am quite content to watch the Nile flow past my window. You see, in many ways, I am only biding my time. One day soon, it will be my last life, and I will know it. But it is not over yet, and so, I must carry on living and breathing in some way.

A vampire? Most certainly not! Vampires came much after me. I have had the pleasure of brow-beating Dracula in his lair, but that is a tale to savour another time. What you could equate me with is a parasite. I live alongside my host, feasting and abstaining as per my requirements. Naturally, my will overrules his in matters that are important to my survival, but mostly, the host isn't even aware that I am living within. Now, isn't that a much happier existence? A co-existence, if you will.

Take this body. It is of a gentleman of considerable means, a New York stockbroker from the 1930s. I met him here on his honeymoon. Rather charming young woman he was married to, and I... ahem... he tried to keep her happy for the forty-odd years they were together. Although she never understood why his sexual appetite declined so much after the honeymoon — but women didn't probe too deeply into such matters back then. He never remarried, preferring to wander the globe instead, eliciting much sympathy for his widower status.

Settling here was more my choice than his, but by then our wills were so intertwined that I doubt he would have chosen otherwise. As his cognitive abilities have degenerated, I have had to make up the shortfall. Therefore, you will find that although this body is very weak, my mind is as sharp as ever.

Ah! I see an expression flit across your face. Is that when you first suspected? When you saw me hobbling through *Khan el-Khalili* looking for my next victim? No, no, I meant host, of course. Ah! I did not spot you then, you camouflaged yourself well. Yet, the next time you couldn't help but approach me. And here you are!

How are the *koftas*? Do have some more. They will go off other-wise, and I hate waste.

Where was I? Oh yes, about the information I was siphoning to my grandfather. Today, you might call him a double-agent, but back then he served two masters as a matter of course. Quite a few of his peers did as well. One was the pharaoh and the other, the priesthood. A very delicate position, you must understand, and a tenuous one too. It was like tightrope walking. One misstep and you could plunge to your death.

Now, I was only eleven years old myself, so I understood little of it. All I knew was that grandfather was an important man, even though he was a slave. This may come as a surprise to you, or maybe not, seeing as you are a 'scholar', but slaves in ancient Egypt could hold important positions if they showed themselves as clever, willing and able, and my grandfather certainly did.

One day, a few weeks before my master's death, I was summoned to my grandfather's house for dinner. The pharaoh allowed me monthly visits to my family, and the summons coincided with my day off.

"Sit here, boy." Grandfather commanded, as I was served delicacy after delicacy. Not knowing that this was his way of fattening the calf before the slaughter, I ate happily, chatting and revealing further tidbits about my master and his political machinations.

When I had eaten my fill and fallen back on the cushions, too stuffed to move, Grandfather leaned in and told me what I had to do.

To say I was shocked might be an understatement. See how I still get goosebumps recalling that conversation?

"Why?" I remember asking him, trembling in fear. Pragmatic as always, he said that since one party was paying far more than the other, it was to his benefit to perform their bidding. "But what of me?" I questioned him then, fearing what my betrayal would cost me...

. . .

You must stop interrupting me because it takes forever then to pick up the thread of my narrative. What is it you ask? Was I colluding in the death of my king? I suppose I was. But was I really? As an eleven-year-old, how much agency do you think I had?

Anyway, to return to that awful evening, I remember begging my grandfather not to go ahead with this terrible plan. I remember offering to trade my life for my master's. See how loyal I was even then! Little did I know how it would come back to bite me.

My part, initially, was just to leave the door to the pharaoh's bedchamber unlocked, and to make myself scarce. But even as I offered my life in place of the pharaoh's, I saw a gleam in my grandfather's eyes.

"Yes!" He whispered excitedly. "Yes, you will sacrifice yourself, but not for him. For us. If you kill yourself, no suspicion will fall upon your family."

And so, my fate was sealed.

You look so sad now. Really, don't be. Do you not think I did well out of it? I am tired; it is true, but how much I have experienced in the multiple lives that I have lived! Far more than a young slave boy in Egypt could have ever envisioned. You may not believe this, but I have been responsible for many of the events that have steered history too. When I have wanted to, I have wielded power through the host I've chosen to inhabit. At other times, I have preferred the anonymity of the ordinary existence — watching, as a bystander might, events unfold; their effects rippling through the fabric of time.

I have had companions and antagonists, friends and foes, followers and challengers, through the myriad journeys I have undertaken.

I have been witness to the rise of the Ancient Greek civilisation and the fall of the Roman Empire. I have walked in the footsteps of the Buddha, philosophised with Confucius, ridden with Alexander the Great, stacked stones for the Great Wall of China, watched the crucifixion of Jesus and the birth of Mohammed. Through crusades and conquests, plagues and wars, I have carried on living and walking.

I have been Genghis Khan and Machiavelli, Liberace and Proust. I have been everything and nothing, catalyst and powder keg.

Do close your mouth now. A mother in another life once told me I'd catch flies that way. I see you are astounded beyond measure now. You could talk to me all evening, all lifetime even, and still not know a fraction of what I know. But neither of us has that kind of time, do we?

One lesson, you ask? Ha! Ha! Ha! Just one?

Very well, if there was just one lesson I could impart, it would be to look at the future with one eye firmly fixed on the past. Everything is cyclical. It comes around again and again, and if you are perceptive enough, you will recognise the patterns. Although I do believe I waste my breath. Humankind is too arrogant, too drunk on its supposed superiority to recognise its own fallibility.

Once it was decided, there was no more discussion to be had. As head of the household, Grandfather held the key to all our fates. That my life had been deemed as dispensable was something my family accepted without a murmur. As it was, I was much closer to the pharaoh than I had ever been to my kith and kin.

On the chosen day, I left the door to the bedchamber unlocked, as directed. Meant to be away on an errand, I chose instead to hide and watch how they killed my master.

Why, you ask? Why not? If my life and death were to be so closely tied to his, do you not think it was my right to witness his death?

The queen went into labour the same night, and in the hubbub that ensued, the pharaoh's death almost went unnoticed. It was I who raised the alarm, I who wept like a baby as guards rushed in from all quarters, I who felt personally responsible when the queen's child was still-born, and I who vowed to her in her bloody birth-chamber that my life and my death were for my pharaoh.

Dramatic, you sneer. Naturally. You are a modern man. Your feelings are superficial and temporary, your affections easily transferred. What could you possibly understand of love?

Yes, love. If it is not transparently clear to you by now, then I must spell it out. I didn't just love my master, I was in love with him.

The queen perhaps saw it then, or maybe she had always known. At any rate, it convinced her of my innocence. But what my grandfather had not reckoned with was her power. You see, the queen was formidable in her piety and none other than Anuket, the goddess of the river Nile, had blessed her with the ability to cast the most powerful spells.

In her grief and anger, she cursed the conspirators to eternal damnation - *Hom Dai* - while blessing me alongside that I could rise up and smite whosoever disturbed her beloved husband's eternal resting place. The dagger I drove through my heart was one that she had given me, making me the recipient of a boon and a bane. As I was partially responsible for her husband's demise, my powers were cursed too. Quite how mixed that blessing was I wouldn't find out until it was too late.

Shall we clear up here? No, there's no need to wash up. Just take the dishes to the sink, my cleaner will do the rest. Did you enjoy your meal? I see you've left nothing on your plate. That is always a good sign, and a compliment to your host.

Let us have some *basbousa* as dessert. Do not look so alarmed, it is only semolina cake, and not as sweet as the dates do not worry! You have been doing so well until now, indulge me for a little longer. I would offer you tea, but we are still working through the claret, are we not?

Look how the lights of the marina twinkle in the distance. I have the same view from my bedroom. I fall asleep to their glow and wake up to the sunlight reflecting off the pyramids in the distance.

Where was my master buried? In the Valley of the Kings -*Wadi El Melouk*, but of course. Where else? I will not pinpoint the exact location to you. Enough harm has come of that already. But as I told you, he was buried with sufficient riches, vestments, food and wine to take him on his journey to the afterlife.

My grave, on the other hand, remained unmarked deliberately. With the powerful curse that I held within me, any disturbance to the pharaoh's casket would mean crossing over me first. The queen had ensured it, but in her sagacity, she placed multiple hexes in the hieroglyphics inscribed upon the inner and outer chamber walls of the tomb. This was enough to frighten the more faint-hearted of grave robbers.

Every so often, a more emboldened and hardened criminal would try to gain access, but her powerful spells saw him dispatched with enough sound and fury to strike fear into any other band foolhardy enough to want to try.

In this manner, we remained undisturbed for many, many years.

Ah, I see you liked the *basbousa*! Good, good. Let us return to the living room. Excuse my coughing. These lungs are unused to quite as much talking as I have done today.

Who was it that breached the tomb and stole my master's death mask?

Have you heard of the saying - 'Fools rush in where angels fear to tread'? Of course you have! A countryman of yours coined it.

Picture this: an itinerant thief, a man of such little value that his own tribe disowns him, accidentally chances upon the entrance to a corridor leading to the tomb. Somehow, and I can only ascribe it to dumb luck, he makes it past all of the queen's curses and enters the sanctum sanctorum. There, he is so awestruck by the riches that greet him, that he stuffs his bags full, throwing his companion, a mangy cat he carries in a cloth on his shoulder, to one side. He ransacks my master's tomb, pulling the death mask off the wooden coffin, his dirty, grubby fingers rifling through everything.

He does not see me rise silently at my pharaoh's feet, so engrossed is he in looting and plundering. But he turns just as I speak my curse. He falls to his death, clutching all the gold he has only had a few moments of his ignominious existence to enjoy.

Why are you silent? Have I painted such a vivid picture that you cannot speak? It is true, even if it sounds unbelievable. Come now, tell me what is on your mind. Why do you doubt me?

Ahh, I see!

You wonder how I lived when he died.

That question haunted me for the longest time, too. I thought that the queen's benediction had given me the power to destroy anyone who bothered the pharaoh's resting place, but if you remember, she had cursed everyone responsible for his death to eternal damnation. In my instance, the curse warped itself into eternal life, a damnation of sorts. Once I had risen, I could not return. My soul latched on to the only living thing in there, and that happened to be the thief's cat.

You look perplexed. I assure you, animals have souls. This cat's soul was a particularly vicious one too, and it did not take kindly to an interloper. It has taken several centuries for me to develop the skills of a persuasive house guest. Back then, I was flailing around, trying to grasp the import of my predicament.

Luckily for me, this cat also had an uncanny ability to survive. Once it found its way back to civilisation, I slowly came to terms with my situation. In fits and starts, I tested my powers, first overcoming the cat's resistance to me, and then subsuming his will to mine. Remember, I carried within me my grandfather's mastery at adaptation. It did not take long after that to figure the rest out.

What happened to my pharaoh's tomb? As soon as I could, and as soon as my next host would allow it, I returned and buried all evidence of its existence. Every few hundred years, a sandstorm would reveal a new passage, and the tomb raiders would return, slowly stripping away everything except for my king's body that still lay mummified within his golden casket, camouflaged within the three other wooden coffins that nobody bothered to pry open.

Why did the queen's hieroglyphic curses work no longer? Perhaps the years leached them of their effectiveness, or perhaps my absence robbed them of their potency. At any rate, once the initial breach had occurred, fear of curses didn't keep anyone out any longer.

However, every time a breach occurred, a searing pain would besiege me, the faces of the culprits branded into my mind's eye. There was power still in the old curse, and until I found and destroyed the perpetrators, I would find no peace, no matter which part of the world I lived in.

It became my mission to seek and destroy all those who disrespected my master's tomb. "The Curse of the Pharaohs," they call it, and now you know just how much truth lies behind that legend.

You look sleepy now. Have I really bored you that much? Why are you examining your wine glass? Do you think I put something in it? But you're the one who has been pouring the wine. You saw the bottles weren't tampered with; you opened them yourself. Then why that look of suspicion?

Come sit down, we are now at the most interesting part of the story.

As you know, my pharaoh's tomb was all but emptied of its treasures over the centuries. In time, no one bothered to raid it any more, seeing as it was an empty shell of its former glorious self. Nature took its course and layer upon layer of sand buried the entrances and tunnels, consigning my master's burial ground to history and legend.

What did I do in the meantime? I wandered the earth, consumed at first by a desire to avenge and once that was accomplished, bereft at having no purpose remaining. Slowly I came to realise that if this was my fate, then I had to make the most of it.

In time I started to satisfy my curiosity by inhabiting creatures of different lands, learning their social mores, toying with their languages, interfering in their politics at times and holding back at others. Watching humankind evolve as I evolved alongside.

Laughing as Chinese alchemists seeking an elixir of life produced gunpowder instead. Crying a mother's copious tears as the Black Death devastated Europe. Watching as Johannes Gutenberg invented the printing press. Admiring Suleiman the Magnificent as he ruled the Ottoman Empire. Reading Shakespeare's 'Hamlet', sourcing the marble for Emperor Shah Jahan's Taj Mahal, being a bystander to The Boston Tea party, wielding the guillotine in The French Revolution, riding the first steam powered trains, bearing witness to the assassination of Abraham Lincoln by John Wilkes Booth. The telegraph, the telephone, the radio, the aeroplane were all invented in the ages I lived in. I could tell you whether Anastasia was really who she claimed to be, what happened in the Stock Market Crash of 1929, and what made Hitler the man he became. But you're not here for that, are you?

As you can see, I kept myself very busy indeed.

At times, exhausted by humankind's endless capacity for strife, I would retreat into the body of an animal. Cats became my favourite, despite my initial experience with one. In ancient Egypt they were venerated as holy and magical creatures. Do you not think there is something inherently royal about them? A hauteur, an indifference to the human species? This became my solace for several years, punctuating the many human bodies I inhabited.

Animals are simple creatures. Their needs are as few as the next meal and a suitable place to sleep in, perhaps a master that coddles them a bit. Cats can do without the last bit, though. Wandering in and out of people's homes, I still learned plenty. But above all, I learned to loathe my own species.

Avaricious, rapacious and gluttonous for the most part, what is there to admire? Aside from the few exceptional men and women who have walked this earth, what have we as a species really contributed to this planet, our home?

I do believe now that most on that journey to the afterlife will find their hearts weighing less than a piece of coal and be judged accordingly.

Ah, a yawn! I see that you're not interested in my observations. More's the pity, for you may learn something of note.

Can I hurry? It's only 10 p.m., what's the rush?

Very well. Shall we get to your times then? The 20th century?

To be perfectly honest, all my, what you may refer to as "globe-trotting" had nearly made me forget what my true objective had been all along. At this point, I was going through the motions, hoping that this variant of my sentence of eternal damnation would be over soon.

I was back on Wall Street, in fact, on the trading floor of the New York Stock Exchange, when the headache hit with such force that I threw up right there, watching the men surrounding me jump back in alarm. A single image, laser-sharp in its clarity, swam into my consciousness. Other blurry figures surrounded him. But it was him that my mind latched on to. A handsome Englishman in a tweed jacket and khaki shorts, painstakingly chipping away at the earth clinging to the outer caskets of my master.

He had discovered what had lain unknown for centuries. My head thumped as though several West African tribal drummers had suddenly taken up residence inside my skull. At once I knew what needed to be done, but instinctively realised that I would never make it in time.

Could you fetch me some water? My throat feels dry.

Thank you.

You are so riveted by my tale you do not wish to move. This is the point you wanted to come to, correct? Well, we are here now. Yes, I have meandered a fair bit, but only so that you may understand that it was my destiny that propelled my actions. Perhaps it was the other way round too, who knows? Did the chicken come before or the egg?

I anger you. I see it in the way you clench your jaw. Come now, we are nearly at the end. Surely you can put up with my eccentricities a bit longer.

Getting from America to Egypt was no easy task in those days. I was wealthy, but not enough to fly all the way, even if such a route existed. So, after a hastily cobbled together excuse to my new wife, I set out on the voyage that would lead me to the Englishman who had violated the last bastion of my master's resting place.

That was the toughest part, and the disappointment that lay at the end of it!

To find them all gone; the casket transported to England, the tomb emptied of its royal personage. Oh, you cannot imagine the frenzy I went into, screaming and tearing at my clothes, all vestiges of the civilised man disappearing in the face of my one true purpose having been thwarted!

The local people who nursed me back told me of days of feverish delirium in which I spoke so many tongues that they believed me to be possessed. Bit by bit, I regained consciousness, and with it came a renewed sense of determination. I would follow this man to the ends of the earth if need be, and destroy the hands that had desecrated my pharaoh's last remnants of dignity.

In England he was being fêted for his discovery, lauded for his contribution. And I waited and watched. One opportune moment is all I required, and before long, the opportunity would present itself to me.

Here, I must pause and ask you again. What do you think humans have learned in all the years they have walked this planet? Digging up consecrated land has yielded what, exactly? Knowledge, wisdom, power? So why not leave the dead in peace? Curiosity is not justification enough.

Your grandfather was not content with all that he had discovered. He wanted to travel back to Egypt to unearth more, and for that he needed funds which were in short supply. This is where I came in. As an investor with an enormous interest in archaeology. I was willing to lend him the money, provided he gave me a private showing of the treasure he had unearthed in the Valley of the Kings.

It was the mystery of the century, wasn't it? The disappearance of the boy pharaoh's golden casket, the mummy it contained, and the archaeologist that had found them.

Do not ask how I did it, merely know that I did. The one thing I will tell you is this: your grandfather did not suffer. Until the very last moment, he believed the charade I'd put on for him. As to where I took my master's body, and how I hid it, that no one will ever find out. You have the beautiful wooden caskets in the museum to admire, don't you? Why not be content with that?

Such fire burns in your belly. Did you really think I was unaware of your antecedents? I know you've looked for me all your life, just as your father before you. Maybe I allowed myself to slip up, or maybe my age has finally caught up with me, but here you are, ready to wreak your revenge.

It's the cloud of shame that has hung over your family for the last seventy years, is it not? The whispers of suspicion that your grandfather sold out? That he retired to some South Pacific island with the money he made from the private collector whom he sold the mummy to? That he abandoned his family. That he was spotted in conference with a mysterious American man before his disappearance, lending credence to the rumours that have swirled ever since.

Well, here you are to avenge your family's name, and I understand. Honour and treachery have been the leitmotifs of my own life, so how could I not?

This slow-acting poison you put in the wine is finally taking effect. You thought I didn't notice? I have been drinking the same claret for so many years, even the slightest difference in taste is palpable to me. But I'm quite content to let this body go.

Tell me boy, now that you know the entire tale, do you not think you overlooked one very important detail?

My time has not come yet. It will come, I know. Maybe a few more lifetimes, and then I will leave this land forever. But before then, the last thing I do as I depart this body is latch on to the only living thing present in the room with me.

Ah, it's no good trying to open that door. I locked it quite securely while you were heating the food. There's nothing for it, but to come and sit by my side once again. As you watch the life ebb out of these eyes, get ready to host me in your own.

New year, new you? Prepare for your wish to come true.

5
____

IDOL

"Why are you up here?"

Heejin swung around, expecting to find one of the other trainees behind her, or worst-case scenario, Gyeong, their manager. But there was no one. Had she imagined it?

She'd snuck up onto the roof terrace of the building after the other girls in her room had fallen asleep. This was her time, the only time she got to be alone with her thoughts after a day filled with school, dance lessons, singing and intense practice sessions that didn't end until midnight. Most other trainees just collapsed into their beds afterwards. Not her. The more exhausted her body got, the more her mind went into overdrive. Only this time, these precious ten minutes, helped calm her enough to sleep for five hours before the alarm rang, waking them for another day that was a repeat of the previous one.

She looked down at the twinkling lights of Gangnam, at the people who still walked the streets—the old vendor who pushed his cart into a side street, the lovers that held hands as they walked home, the tourists in search of Seoul's nightlife—and sighed.

A similar sigh echoed near her left shoulder.

"W... who is it?"

She peered into the darkness. No one seemed to be around, but suddenly an amorphous figure materialised out of the gloom and glided towards her.

"W... who are you?" Heejin whispered, goosebumps rising on her arms as she backed away.

The figure stopped a few steps away. She looked around seventeen, the same age as Heejin. Pale, face as round as the moon, dark hair that fell in waves on her shoulders. She stared mournfully at Heejin.

"You really don't know me?"

Heejin looked at her carefully, recognition dawning as she gasped in shock and started trembling.

"Please don't be scared. I just want to talk, I'm so lonely."

"But... but..."

"Can you sit with me a few minutes?"

Heejin nodded and sat on a little stool, watching the other girl settle herself across from her.

It was Byeol, a member of the K-Pop band, **Star-Crossed**. Nine girls who had sung and danced their way to the top of the Billboard charts, they were worshipped in Korea, Japan, China and nearly the entire world by screaming teenage fans. This was what Heejin and the other idol trainees aspired to. The fame and fortune, the glitz and glamour that came with being the biggest female K-Pop band in the world, like **Star-Crossed** had been. This was what kept them toiling daily without respite. Except that Byeol was no longer a part of **Star-Crossed** because, well, she was dead.

Or was she?

"Oh yes, I am dead."

"Then how... how?"

"How am I here? Well, you are full-Korean. You must know about *gwishin*[1]?"

"Are you a *cheonyeo gwishin*[2]?"

"Am I a virgin ghost? Yes, I think I am."

"But why are you here?" Heejin had started calming down, her natural curiosity asserting itself. Byeol didn't seem threatening. At least she wasn't a *dalgyal gwishin*: the egg-shaped ghost that was the deadliest and most frightening of all. Anyone who saw that ghost would definitely die. Byeol just seemed sad. Heejin could cheer her up if she wanted.

Crossing her knees, Heejin leaned forward and regarded Byeol. The lead singer of **Star-Crossed** was a beautiful girl. Her sharp nose, her incredible jawline, the 24-inch waist had all been held up as an example of perfect Korean beauty. At the top of her game , Byeol had died a few months ago in mysterious circumstances, plunging millions of fans worldwide into mourning. Heejin wanted to ask her how she'd died, but that wasn't the cheeriest route to take, perhaps.

Instead, she asked, "Do you miss it?"

"Life?"

"This life."

"As an idol? No, not at all. But I do miss my family. I'm sad that I caused so much sorrow."

Of course! Byeol must have had a family, like Heejin did. An unexpected pang went through her as a vision of her parents and younger sister swam into her mind. She hadn't seen them in nearly two years, and fifteen minutes of daily conversations did not make up for it.

"I miss my family too."

"Leave then. Leave now. Get out!"

Heejin recoiled from the rage in Byeol's voice.

"I don't want to leave! I've wanted this all my life and I'm not giving up on my dream. Other girls miss their families too, we don't just leave because of it."

Byeol nodded slowly, her ghostly body slumping.

"I'm sorry. How can I tell you to leave when I didn't? You are chasing the same mirage that I was."

"Would you like to see some of my moves?" To distract her, Heejin stood up quickly and started humming and dancing, moving her chest and hips in the sexy manner they had been taught. Her hands skimmed over her small breasts, moved over her tiny waist, and settled on the narrow hips that she shook in rhythm to the absent music.

Byeol watched her, one eyebrow raised. Her foot tapped involuntarily and at one point, she almost smiled.

> *"Watch me, watch me*
> *As I walk away from you*
> *You broke my heart first*
> *Now I'll break yours too*
>
> *I'll be so hot*
> *So hot*
> *You won't be able*
> *To touch me*
> *But you'll want to, want to..."*

Heejin sang as she lost herself in the moment, her body moving in the way it had been trained to.

When she had first auditioned as a twelve year old for the largest K-Pop company in Korea, SP Entertainment, she had been turned away for being too stiff in her moves. Determined to make it as an idol trainee, she had taken singing and dancing lessons, learning how to move her body in the calculatedly sinuous manner of the idols. Provocative and naïve, innocent and sexy, untouched but still available as a fantasy—all the things demanded of a K-Pop idol—did not come naturally to her. But she had persisted, and here she was, on the brink of fame.

"You know that is one of **Star-Crossed**'s songs, don't you?"

"Yes, I do. We practice to it all the time." Heejin smiled at Byeol, no longer bothered that she was sharing the roof with the ghost of a former idol. Company was company, and making friends in the cutthroat environment of idol training had been tricky.

"Byeol?"

"Hmm?"

"Why are you here?"

"Unfinished business."

"What kind of unfinished business?"

"Isn't it time for bed? You have to wake up in four hours."

Heejin stopped dancing immediately, realising that she had a long day ahead and needed her sleep.

"Will you be here tomorrow?"

"I am here every day."

With a quick wave, she flew down the steps to the dormitory she shared with three other trainees. Slipping into the room noiselessly, she slid under her covers, still marvelling at the strange encounter. Tomorrow she would get some answers from Byeol.

The day began at 5 a.m. Sharing one bathroom between four girls wasn't easy. Heejin peered over the head of the shortest girl, trying to brush her teeth as she wondered if it was worth mentioning Byeol to her roommates. In the light of day, the entire episode seemed like a dream. Had she made it all up? Was her mind so tired that she had tripped into some kind of delirium?

At school, she could barely concentrate on her lessons, desperate to get her hands on her phone to google details of Byeol's life and death.

"Heejin, where are you? You have been daydreaming all day long!" Minji asked her on the way back to their dorms.

"Oh, nothing. I'm just a little tired, that's all."

"Tired? I'm exhausted! Weigh-in is tomorrow and I've been living on cucumber and ice cubes. I cannot weigh over 50 kilograms..."

As Minji prattled on, Heejin thanked her good genes that weight was never a cause of worry for her. Naturally skinny, the rigorous daily routine didn't let an extra millimetre of fat stick to her bones.

"What do you think?" Minji was waiting for her response, so Heejin shrugged, hoping that would be sufficient.

"Well, I believe she does. The other evening I saw her sneak out for a *bananamat uyu*.[3] So she said, but I think there's a boyfriend. If Gyeong finds out..." She let the threat hang in the air.

Heejin closed her eyes for a moment. She really didn't care about the love lives of the other trainees. The rules were clear. No boys, no dating. In fact, their dorms were located far away from the male trainees for that very reason. Minji was getting on her nerves now.

"Should we change? Practice begins in half an hour."

They both hurried up to their dorm, walking past the larger hall that slept Group 3. The top two groups had been given the smaller dorms with four beds each. Group 3 had twenty-four girls and twelve bunk beds between them. Heejin lowered her eyes as she walked past. She felt sorry for these trainees. It was only a matter of time before they were culled.

No one was guaranteed a debut, and even though she was in Group 1, one poor performance could see her sidelined. The competition was intense, but all of them knew that at the end of these arduous days, if they got picked to form a K-Pop group, the entire world would be at their feet.

Gyeong walked into their dorm as they were changing.

"Girls, the big boss is coming to see you today. Put on some makeup and do your hair nice, okay?"

She was trembling with nervousness, her usually high-pitched voice even higher than normal.

"Is he coming to make the selection?" Sun Hee asked in a manner so audacious that all of them looked at her open-mouthed.

"Chairman Ji Hwan is coming. That is all I know, and that is all you need to know. Now, get ready and come downstairs soon."

As soon as Gyeong left, the speculation began.

Aside from Heejin, Minji and Sun Hee, the fourth member of their dorm was the quiet and shy Yeon.

"Yeon, baby, this could be your chance to show them what you've got." Minji teased her. "If they like what they see, you could end up as the visual."

"Why her?" Sun Hee snorted.

"You mean, why not you?"

"No, I mean why her? She's only fifteen, and she has a sweet voice, but didn't Gyeong say the other day that she needs a bit of her jaw shaved?"

"Ah, you would know, wouldn't you Sun Hee?"

Heejin intervened before it turned into another cat fight between them.

"Come on! We don't have much time."

As each of them curled their hair and applied their makeup, Heejin considered her own face in the mirror. She wasn't classically beautiful like Sun Hee, nor did she have a shock of blonde hair like Minji. She couldn't sing as sweetly as Yeon either. But what she had was determination, comportment, and attitude. In Chuncheon where she'd grown up, people had often remarked that she had star presence. She could make a room full of people stop eating their *mak-kuk-soo* [4] when she sang and danced. This was even before she'd begun any lessons. For Heejin, there had never been another life. This life had chosen her.

Downstairs, they were herded into the large dance studio where they practiced daily. All the girls had made an effort and for a moment Heejin felt as though she was seeing dozens of pretty dolls reflected in the mirrors that lined the far wall, each a clone of the other. Then she shook her head, and the illusion disappeared.

Gyeong opened the door and let a squad of men in. Chairman Ji Hwan was dressed in his usual black suit and red tie, but the three men that followed him were casually dressed. One even had a ponytail.

They sat on the chairs placed by the wall and took out little notebooks and pencils. One of them nodded at Gyeong, and then she turned the music on.

The opening strains of "Hiccup" floated in the air, and they took up their positions. In no time at all, they were all moving and miming to the music, their bodies gyrating in rhythm, their sexy-cute personas bending, shaking, pirouetting.

Heejin could not stop smiling. She was born to perform, to be here, to be chosen.

～

"It wasn't a showcase."

"Then?"

"Chairman Ji Hwan had brought some investors to watch us perform."

"Ah yes, the investors." Byeol stared down at the lights of Gangnam that half-lit her beautiful profile. Heejin had told her all about her day, but Byeol had barely spoken, just nodding in the right places.

"You were a trainee here, weren't you, Byeol?" Heejin couldn't contain her questions anymore.

"Yes, I was." Byeol smiled sadly. Then she turned towards Heejin. "I was even younger than you when I was selected. Only twelve. When I left home, I felt like I had cut my heart out and left it behind. But everyone told me how lucky I was, and I believed them."

"But you were lucky! Who wouldn't want the life of an idol? You get to be a singer, a dancer, an actress. Everyone looks up to you. You get to live in Hannam the Hill, with views of the Han river and Mount Namsan. Who wouldn't want this life?"

Then she looked at Byeol's face and shut up.

"Did Chairman Ji Hwan like any of the girls today?"

Heejin felt another sharp stab of envy as she remembered him calling Yeon aside to talk to her.

"Yes," she nodded, "Yeon. But she has the sweetest voice out of all of us."

"How old is she?"

"Yeon? She is fifteen. Why?"

"You have to do something for me." Byeol's voice had grown harsh, her words tripping over each other. "Tell Yeon she must not go out with them. Tell her to complain of a stomachache, of anything; any illness. Get her to make it up. She must not go out. Do you understand?"

"Yes, yes. I understand. She must not go out. But she didn't go anywhere. She came back to the dormitory with us."

"Tell her, anyway."

Suddenly, all the urgency left her, and Byeol seemed to deflate. Heejin moved closer and put her arm around Byeol's shoulders, but her limb just passed through the mist of Byeol's body.

"Oh, I forgot you are a *gwishin!*"

"Heejin?"

"Hmmm?"

"You know this life of luxury you are dreaming of?"

"Yes?"

"It's not like that in the beginning at all. It takes years to pay off the company's debts. Whatever money the group makes, the company takes 90% of it, leaving you to share the 10% between you. Once you have split the money and repaid your debt, there really isn't all that much left. It can take years to achieve this fantasy life."

"Still," Heejin sighed, "what's a few years? I'm only seventeen."

"I debuted at seventeen too. It took me nearly seven years to pay off my debts."

"But then look at the life you led! Travelling and performing all over the world, lead actress in a television show..." Heejin paused. "Wait! You are twenty-four?"

"Twenty-six actually."

"But... but... you look so young!"

"I always looked younger than my age."

"Byeol?"

"Yes?"

"What happened to you?"

"It's not what happened to me that's important, it's what happened to Ah-In."

"Who is Ah-In?"

Byeol stayed silent and lost in her thoughts. Heejin cleared her throat.

"Ah-In," Byeol spoke softly, "was like a sister to me. She was beautiful, and she sang and danced like a dream."

"Where is she? Did she not get selected in the showcase?"

"No, she did not. After five years of training, she was sent home."

"Why?"

"Because they found out that she liked girls."

"What do you mean? I like girls too. How is that bad?"

"Not in the way she liked them. Like a boyfriend."

"Oh."

Heejin had heard of women like that, women who liked other women in that way. Women who never married because they did not want to be with a man.

"Was she... did she... like you in that way?"

"What? No! I told you, she was like a sister to me. But Ah-In did not have a loving family to return to. She had never been good at studies, and once she was kicked out of training, she had nothing to fall back on."

"What happened to her?"

"She ended up on the streets, Heejin."

"You mean..."

"Yes, she became a sex-worker." Byeol's shoulders shook as she cried ghostly tears. "Years later, when I was living in that fancy house on the hill that you dream of, she came to see me."

"And?"

"She wanted money, she was desperate. But I could see that the money was for drugs. By then Ah-In looked so old and thin - her ribs stuck out from under her T-shirt. There were needle marks all over her arms. I tried to get her to stay with me, to get her treatment..." Byeol stopped and swallowed hard. "But she left, cursing me because I wouldn't give her any money."

She turned and looked into Heejin's eyes.

"Tell me, if it all goes wrong, will you be able to return to your family?"

Heejin thought of her father's kind face, her mother's soft hands, her sister's cheeky grin, and nodded.

"Yes."

"Good." Byeol sighed. "That's good."

"What happened to Ah-In?"

"I don't know, Heejin. Who knows what happens to people who live in the shadows? She may still be alive or she may be dead. All I know is that the Ah-In I loved died the day they kicked her out of here."

"She's fainted!"

Heejin had heard the thump while they were rehearsing, but hadn't turned around for fear of being scolded by Gyeong. Training was sacred, and nothing and nobody could interrupt it. Now the music was turned off, and they turned to see who the latest casualty was.

It was Minji.

Gyeong called her and Yeon over.

"She is your roommate. Pick her up and take her to the dorm. Stay with her till she wakes up. Then return to the practice."

They nodded and went towards the collapsed girl.

"You take her legs," Heejin directed, "I'll take her arms."

Between them they carried the deadweight of Minji towards their dorm. Settling her into bed, they waited for her to regain consciousness.

"She hasn't been eating much," Yeon remarked softly.

"I know. She's worried she might be overweight."

They looked at the slight girl on the bed, noting the shadows under her eyes and her sunken cheeks. When Minji was awake, her face was always so animated it was easy to forget how gaunt she had become.

"Yeon," Heejin suddenly remembered her conversation from the previous night, "did Chairman Ji Hwan ask you to go out anywhere?"

Yeon looked startled. She looked around before whispering, "He said I had a sweet voice and that maybe, I'd like to sing to the sponsors one day?"

"No! Don't do it. Promise me you won't."

"I was not going to. Heejin, can I tell you something?"

"Yes?"

"I don't want to do this anymore."

"Really?"

"All I ever wanted to do was sing. I don't like the rest of it - the dancing, the performing. I am not like Sun Hee or even you. All the girls here, they like the limelight. I hate it!"

"Then what are you going to do?"

"My training ends in another month. I will decline their contract and return home."

"And your debts?"

"If they don't sign me, I don't owe them anything."

Heejin regarded the young girl sitting next to her. Yeon seemed determined and far wiser than she had ever given her credit for. At least she knew what she wanted. Increasingly, Heejin found that she herself didn't.

"Unnhhhh..." Minji groaned before opening her eyes. "What happened?"

"You fainted," Heejin supplied.

"Not again!" She sat up, rubbing her head.

"Minji, you have to eat!" Yeon looked worried.

"Eat? Are you crazy? I even spit out my saliva before I get weighed!"

"Why are you ruining your health this way?" Yeon pleaded.

"Because she really, really wants it!" Sun Hee sauntered in. "And you know what, even though I don't like you Minji, I admire your guts."

Minji glared at Sun Hee. "Then why are you taking so many chances with your own training?"

"What do you mean?"

"All that sneaking out to drink banana milk! You think I don't know that you have a boyfriend?"

Sun Hee's face paled, and she sat down on the bed abruptly.

"Shut up! You don't know anything. Don't be spreading rumours about me."

Heejin looked from one girl to the other. The air crackled with their animosity.

"Please, stop! Life is hard enough without us fighting amongst ourselves. Sun Hee, why are you here?"

"Gyeong sent me to fetch you."

"Then, let's go! Minji, you'll be okay?"

"Yes, yes. Go, I'll be fine." Minji said, weariness lacing her voice as she turned to a side, her back to them.

In the studio, the girls were still practicing, this time to another of **Star-Crossed**'s songs - 'Stalker'. The moves for this weren't the usual girly K-pop manoeuvres. The song had originally been written for the biggest K-pop boy band, **Anti**, but had eventually been rejected by them, finding its way to the largest K-pop girl band. With back flips and splits, cartwheels and body rolls, the choreography was more hip hop and athletic than the usual songs they practiced to. Heejin remembered how the girls of **Star-Crossed** had kicked and punched into the camera, bringing an entirely new vibe to the otherwise ultra-feminine band.

"I see you everywhere
Hiding behind the walls
You chase my every breath
At night, I hear you call

You are my dream
My nightmare

My horror
My fantasy

You are my stalker
My chaser
My trapper
My hawker

But I'll get you
Before you get me
Yes, I'll get you
Before you get me..."

Yeon, Heejin and Sun Hee joined in seamlessly, their moves mimicking the other girls'. It was nearly 7 p.m. but no one dared mention dinner to Gyeong. Only once she was satisfied that they had done their best would they get a break.

Heejin looked around at the thirty-odd girls in the room. How many of them would make it to the final selection? The company had already indicated that they were looking for a six-member girl group. Twenty-six of them would have to be culled. What would happen to those who didn't make it? Would they try their luck as trainees elsewhere, would they return home or, God forbid, turn to the streets like Ah-In?

Suddenly, they heard a commotion from a corner of the room. Gyeong was laying into someone. They all stopped mid-move to listen.

"You are useless! You cannot speak Korean well and you cannot dance. I will talk to Chairman Ji Hwan to have you removed immediately!"

It was Lamai, the Thai trainee who had joined them eight months ago. A quiet, hardworking girl, Heejin had often seen her bent over her books practicing writing and speaking Korean. But it had probably not been good enough for Gyeong, who was famously intolerant of foreigners.

Hadn't Byeol been half-Japanese too? Had she been treated just as badly?

Heejin looked at Lamai's downcast face as Gyeong carried on upbraiding her and felt sorry for the girl. It was hard enough leaving one's family to move far away, let alone leaving one's country for another. If all one got was abuse and hostility, was it really worth it?

"You are half-Japanese, aren't you? I remember reading that in The Kraze Magazine." Heejin sat on her favourite stool on the roof terrace.

"Yes, I am, or I was. Now I'm nothing."

Momentarily distracted by this, Heejin looked at Byeol intently.

"There are so many things I want to ask you, like what happened to you, how did you die... I tried googling that but there was no information. But first, what did you mean by 'unfinished business'?"

"You are a curious one!" Byeol smiled. "Tell me, when is the final selection?"

"You haven't answered any of my questions!"

"I will, in good time. Now, when is the final selection?"

"The showcase is next week on Friday."

"And how many girls will be picked?"

"They've said six."

"What are your chances?"

"I am in Group 1, so pretty good, I think. Sun Hee is determined to be the visual, and I think they want Yeon as the voice. I'll just be happy to debut."

"Did you talk to Yeon as I asked?"

"Yes, well..." Heejin lowered her voice to a whisper. "She actually wants to leave. She says that this life is not for her. Can you imagine?"

Byeol slumped back as if in relief. A small smile played about her lips, and when she looked up at Heejin, her eyes were gleaming.

"Then my unfinished business is finished." Her smile widened, but then twisted into a frown. "What am I to do about you?"

"What do you mean?"

"I could go now, but you... I've grown fond of you and I cannot leave you without changing your mind."

"Byeol!" Heejin cried out in exasperation. "You always talk in riddles and I understand nothing!"

"My little Heejin," Byeol came and sat by her side, "don't get annoyed. I will not be here for a while now, but I promise to return next Friday after the showcase. Meet me up here and I'll explain everything."

Heejin nodded and swallowed. It was the best she was going to get, and who was she to argue with a *gwishin*?

She missed her evening sessions with Byeol. Coming up to the roof terrace and sitting on her own wasn't restful anymore, now that her sounding board had disappeared. She hoped Byeol would return, but what guarantee was there that she would?

Heejin was smart enough to piece together that Byeol's 'unfinished business' was dissuading at least one girl from continuing on the idol path. Now that Yeon, directly or indirectly, had been influenced into giving up on the idol dream, Byeol could probably head off to wherever *gwishin* went once they were done haunting the living.

If Heejin were to examine her own feelings about being a K-pop idol, she knew that they were mixed. Byeol had taken off the rose-tinted spectacles that Heejin had viewed this life with, but that did not shake her resolve in the slightest. She knew the pitfalls, but she still wanted the idol life. Heejin was a born performer, and no other life could give her the satisfaction that this one did.

The final week of rehearsals was frenzied and everything had been ratcheted up. They were rotated through various performances, assessed on their singing, their dancing, their emoting skills. Each girl was primed to perform; to give the showcase event her best shot.

On Wednesday evening, Sun Hee announced that she was going for a stroll just after dinner. Minji immediately planted herself at the door to their dorm.

"No! You're not going anywhere. I don't care what you do, but you are not jeopardising our chances. If Gyeong finds out that we knew…"

Sun Hee smirked at her. "I'm only going out to get some fresh air. What's your problem?"

"You know we are not allowed boyfriends! I'm not moving. You can do what you want after Friday, but until then you follow the rules like the rest of us."

"Don't be ridiculous! Get out of my way."

Sun Hee tried to push past her, but Minji was stronger than she looked and pushed back with equal force.

Before long, they were screaming and kicking one another, pulling at the other's hair, trying to claw each other's face. Heejin tried separating them while Yeon uttered calming words, but they were not willing to listen.

Just then, Gyeong walked in.

"What's going on here?"

The girls immediately stopped fighting and stood up from the floor, dusting off their clothes.

"I asked what's going on?"

Minji glared at Sun Hee as if daring her. Sun Hee darted a quick glance at Gyeong, then lowered her eyes and muttered, "*Unnie*,[5] I was just going for a stroll…"

Gyeong looked at the state of the girls and then remarked brusquely, "Go tidy yourself before going for your stroll, Sun Hee."

Then she turned and left the room. Sun Hee flicked a triumphant look at Minji and headed towards the bathroom.

After she had left, Minji shrugged helplessly. "I was just trying to protect all of us - even her, that stupid *aish*[6]!"

Yeon took her hand and led her to the bed.

"Minji, I've wanted to tell you for a while, but wasn't sure if I should…"

Heejin went over and sat across from them on her own bed. Yeon stroked Minji's hand as she spoke softly.

"Sun Hee doesn't have a boyfriend. She goes to visit Chairman Ji Hwan."

Minji's mouth opened and closed like a fish, but no words came out. Heejin felt a violent shiver run through her.

"H… how do you know?" She asked the fifteen-year-old.

"She told me herself. The Chairman has promised her that she will be the face of the group. Her debut is assured."

They sat together in silence, absorbing the words Yeon had imparted.

Close to 1 a.m. the door to their dorm opened silently and Sun Hee slipped in. None of the girls moved, even though they weren't asleep. They listened to her climb into bed; they heard the bedsprings squeak as she settled in, and then her soft snores as she fell asleep almost immediately.

Something fundamental had changed. They dared not speak of the secret that weighed heavily on them, but just as Sun Hee had fallen in their estimation, Yeon had risen inversely.

Now even Minji knew that Yeon had no intention of staying, and her reasons for it. She didn't say much to her, but treated her with the sort of respect one accorded to elders.

"She is an old soul," she whispered to Heejin on the morning of the showcase. "Too good to be a part of this world."

Yeon had already started packing her things. She came up to them and gave them a hug. They hugged her back, wishing her well. Then she turned to Sun Hee, who was sitting on her bed, knees clasped to her chest.

"Sun Hee, I will leave this morning, but before I go, I just wanted to say that you must believe in yourself. You are beautiful and talented, and deserve your success."

Then she picked up her case and left the room in search of Gyeong.

Heejin and Minji stared at the door as she shut it behind her. They had always known that eventually their numbers would dwindle, but losing Yeon hurt much more than they could have imagined. They heard a soft sob and turned around. Sun Hee was rocking back and forth, crying. In silent agreement, they went to sit on either side of her and put their arms around her.

"Shhh," Minji whispered, "not today. We have to go out and conquer! Put your warrior face on, Sun Hee."

Chairman Ji Hwan sat in the front of the room with three other men, presumably the producers; a petite woman they had never seen before and Gyeong, their manager, beside them.

As they went through their routines, Heejin noticed Gyeong passing notecards on to the Chairman, who would write something on them and then set them aside. One producer would then make his own notes and give it to the next man. The woman sitting with them watched the girls intently, ignoring the notes that were being passed back and forth.

Before each routine, they were called forward to introduce themselves. After each routine, the names that were omitted had to leave the studio. With Yeon having left, their own future seemed uncertain. She had been the most naturally talented singer amongst them, and secretly Heejin had always believed that it was because they complemented her so well that Minji, Sun Hee and she had ended up in Group 1.

Eventually there were only twelve girls left in the studio - the three of them, two others from Group 2, and seven from Group 3. They stood shuffling their feet as the judging panel conferred amongst themselves. A few times Chairman Ji Hwan's eyes flicked towards Sun Hee, but his expression remained neutral.

Then the strains of **Star-Crossed**'s "Watch Me" came on, and the girls started moving in synchronisation, each one singing a few lines before letting the next girl take over. Heejin remembered singing and dancing to the song in front of Byeol on the first night they had met. How had Byeol felt at her final evaluation? Had she been worried and upset over Ah-In, or had she given it her all?

Heejin knew everything depended upon this moment, upon how she performed, upon whether she was compelling enough. All her doubts vanished and she let her inner entertainer emerge. Suddenly, everything around her blurred and disappeared - the studio, the girls, the producers, Gyeong... It was just her and the music. Her body swayed in rhythm, the lyrics flowing from her as though they had been written by her own hands. For one moment, she thought she saw Byeol in the mirror, but that image dissolved and all she saw were the bright lights of the stage, and all she heard was the thunderous applause from the audience.

And then, even that didn't matter.

Her soul seemed to leave her body as she danced. She felt larger than herself, more beautiful, more powerful; as though the earth itself was urging her to move and the wind itself was swaying along to the music. In some sort of perfect splintering, it felt like she was living the experience twice over - as a performer and as a watcher. She saw herself enunciate the lyrics, watched her body move in tandem, her limbs exquisite, her expression one of sheer ecstasy. In that moment, she felt complete and in perfect harmony with her destiny.

When the song ended, her body juddered to a halt. Everyone was looking at her, awestruck. She blinked. What had just happened? Had she made a fool of herself?

Sun Hee looked furious, but Minji winked at her, mouthing a quick "well done". Gyeong consulted with Chairman Ji Hwan and then stood up to address them.

"All of you have done well. Now, you must leave the studio and wait outside. We will call you back when we have made our decision. I have laid out some watermelon for you to snack on. Please go out and have some."

They trooped out, exhausted and hungry. Minji grabbed Heejin's hand, pulling her to a side.

"What happened in there?"

"What do you mean?"

"You sang and danced as if you were possessed! I could swear it was as if **Star-Crossed** was performing in front of us!"

"I don't remember much. It felt as though my body was floating in the air. I've never felt like that before."

"I tell you Chairman Ji Hwan was impressed. He kept goggling at you as if he had never seen you before."

"Why was Sun Hee glaring at me, then?"

"She's never seen you as competition before, that's why."

"That's silly, we are all in a competition here."

"Yes, but aside from Yeon, Sun Hee has always considered herself the star of the show. You shook her confidence today."

"But she'll still get selected... Yeon said... you know, because of..."

"Yes, I know." Minji chewed on her lip for a bit. "Still, it's good that she knows you can out-perform her anytime. It will keep her nose out of the air!"

"So you are in the band?" Byeol murmured behind her.

Heejin had been waiting on the roof terrace for twenty minutes, losing hope of ever seeing Byeol again. She swung around to face the *cheonyeo gwishin.*

Byeol stood behind her, at once transparent but also shimmering with some kind of inner light. Where had she gone for the past week, and how had she returned?

"I know," Byeol sighed, "you have so many questions, and you have been patient. So, tonight I will answer them for you. Come, sit by me."

Wordlessly, Heejin went over and sat on her favourite stool. She knew this was the last time she'd be here. The roof terrace wouldn't be the same without Byeol.

"What happened to you?"

"I killed myself."

Heejin gasped. She had suspected it, but to hear it vocalised seemed almost too cruel.

"But why? You had it all!"

"Heejin, have you not been listening to me? I had nothing, none of us do. It took me several years to realise it, and then, when I did... it was the only way out."

"H... How did...?"

"How did I do it? Does it matter? There are a million different ways if you go looking for them."

"But the news..."

"Yes, it was hushed up. You can see for yourself how powerful these management companies are. For SP Entertainment, losing their star performer in this manner would have been too much of a scandal. So, they allowed rumours to take over the truth."

"The drug rumours."

"Yes, the drug overdose rumours." Byeol looked beyond her at the Lotte World Tower. "Have you ever looked at that building and wondered how tall it is?"

Thrown off by the sudden switch of topic, Heejin shook her head. She had never been very interested in buildings.

"You know, it is the tallest building in South Korea, but it is only the fifth tallest in the world."

Heejin nodded, confused.

"Fame is a little bit like that. There is always a taller building." Byeol looked at her, her expression sad.

"Are you still trying to put me off?"

"No. I can see that your mind is made up. I'm only here to answer your questions, then I'll leave."

"Forever?"

"Forever."

"About today... the audition... you were there. I saw you."

Byeol smiled. "Is that a question?"

Heejin swallowed and asked her what was really on her mind.

"Did you... somehow... possess me?"

At this, Byeol laughed, showing her small, perfectly even teeth.

"Why would you say that?"

"It's just... when I was performing, I felt strange, like I was leaving my body. I could see myself from the outside, but I could feel myself from the inside, too. Was that you?"

"Heejin, I was there, but only to watch you. Whatever happened to you was your own experience, and had nothing to do with me."

They sat silently for a few minutes, then Byeol started speaking again. The words came out of her in a gush.

"You asked me once what my 'unfinished business' was. I had vowed to myself that before I passed to the other side, I would show at least one girl the ugly side of this business. When you kept coming up here, I picked you as that girl. But now, after Yeon has left, and my original mission has been accomplished, I feel there is still something I must say to you."

"What?" Heejin's voice was small, like a little girl's. Her heart hurt as she felt very alone suddenly.

"There is nothing wrong with what we do—this singing and dancing, this performing—it gives joy to so many people. It fulfils us creatively too. Some, like Yeon and you, are naturally gifted. Others, like Sun Hee and Minji, are trained into becoming performers. But, it's important not to lose sight of your 'why'. If your only motivations are fame and money, then this life is like a gold plated ornament. In time, the varnish will disappear to reveal the rust and decay inside."

Byeol paused, then looked at Heejin carefully.

"Today, I saw something in you. Something that told me that your 'why' isn't what you claim it is. Am I right?"

Heejin thought back to that moment in the auditorium, that moment when everything in her world had aligned perfectly, and nodded.

Byeol continued, "You are doing this for the right reasons, and that will take you far. But remember to hold on to that purity of feeling that's inside you. If you look for approval from the outside, then you'll end up like I did."

Heejin stared at Byeol. Snippets of news items, conversations on online forums, all started falling into place. She was piecing together something she had always known subconsciously.

"It was the *sasaeng* [7]fans, wasn't it?"

"Partly, yes. Those obsessive fans who stalk, follow and monitor every move we make, made life unbearable. It became suffocating and dangerous! One became so infatuated that he broke into my house twice. But you know what was worse?"

"What?"

"Even the fans that supposedly loved me. One average performance, one hair out of place, and the hate they would spew..." Byeol shuddered. "I was called ugly, a plastic surgery wonder, a half-breed talentless *amkae*[8]! No one defended or protected me, and it wore me down. I just couldn't take it anymore."

"Couldn't you have just left? Why take such a drastic step?"

"When you are in as dark a place as I was, all logic and reason abandon you."

"But what about your parents, the other girls in your group? Wasn't there anyone you could turn to?"

Byeol sat silently.

"Now I think that perhaps I could have reached out to my parents. But at that time all I could think of was how disappointed they would have been in me." A rueful smile crossed her face, and then she shrugged. "As for the other girls, each of them was fighting her own battle. We didn't have a wise little owl like Yeon in our group."

Heejin stood up from her stool, suddenly enraged.

"I will not allow that to happen to me! Or to any of the girls in my group."

Byeol's eyebrows rose.

"What are you going to do?"

"I am going to change things. Slowly at first, and then when I have more power, I am going to change everything in the K-Pop world! No more slave contracts, no more starving to fit an ideal, no more plastic surgery!"

"Big words, Heejin, but you are only seventeen. How will you fight an industry?"

"By becoming a part of it and then changing it from the inside."

"Really?"

"Yes, really! Don't underestimate me, Byeol." Heejin's chin rose in defiance, every fibre of her being bristling with determination. At the very core of her, she believed she could do it, no matter how long it took or how arduous the path turned out to be. But first, she needed to learn the rules of the game. Then, she would break them one by one.

"And what if your head is turned by the glitz? What if you forget all these promises you're making tonight?"

"I won't." Heejin looked down at Byeol, her inner resolve solidifying into something intractable. There would be no more Byeols or Yeons, no more Ah-Ins or Lamais. An industry that thrived on factory-producing easily disposable clones would find that these clones had voices, thoughts and identities; that they would no longer be dispensed with or abused that easily. No corporation or manager would control them completely or silence them forever. They would be the ones with the last laugh, and the industry would see that this was just the beginning.

Byeol stood up too, the shimmer on her having increased a thousandfold.

"I wondered, in the beginning, if I had chosen the right girl to talk to. But now I see that I was not guided wrong. If you can do what you say, then my life and my death will not have been wasted."

Heejin looked at Byeol, all her anger evaporating suddenly.

"Byeol, will I truly never see you again?"

"My dear Heejin, who knows?" One gossamer hand reached out and stroked her cheek. "Just remember that my hopes and dreams will travel with you in your life."

There was a noise behind them, and Byeol started fading.

"I have to go now, Heejin. I wish you strength and courage for the long battle ahead..." And just like that, she was gone.

~

"What are you doing up here?" Minji asked as she opened the door to the roof terrace. "I've seen you disappear nearly every evening."

"Oh, nothing," Heejin blinked back her tears, looking out over the architectural landscape of Seoul, "I just come here to gather my thoughts."

"Well, you should be downstairs with us, celebrating! Sun Hee has smuggled in some *Soju*[9]..." Minji grinned.

"I will, in a minute."

"What are you thinking of, anyway? World domination?" Minji laughed.

"K-Pop domination, mostly." Heejin looked her in the eye, deadly serious.

Minji blinked and seemed to sober up. She looked at Heejin and nodded slowly, then said, "Well, if anyone can do it, it's you."

They looked out at the twinkling lights of the city and then, in tacit agreement, turned and walked down the stairs to begin their new life together.

~

6

THE PERFECT WIFE

When Alex Wang divorced his third wife in the summer of 2043, he decided he'd had enough of women. Of human women, that is. He'd tried really hard to make it work with the last one, and they'd kept things going for nearly ten years. But ultimately, it came down to the same old bugbear. She bored him.

Anastasia had been Russian - tall (taller than him), blonde and with a bosom that was the envy of all women in Hong Kong. He'd paid for it, of course. He paid for pretty much everything. It was part and parcel of being the richest man in Southeast Asia.

At the half-century mark in his life, Alex had rid himself of her. She had seemed almost relieved, but the bitch had still wanted more than the eighty-two million dollar settlement that the lawyers had agreed upon. He was glad he was done with her.

Sometimes he still thought back to Chiyon, his first wife and, some might have said, the love of his life. She had been the least trouble of them all. That might have been because she had genuinely loved him, the real him, the man he was before he became THE Alex Wang of Wang Corporation, or WangCo for short. Yet, he'd barely spared her a thought when the time came for an upgrade. Emma, the perfect English rose, first his secretary and then his second wife, had taken Chiyon's place in his life with a breathless urgency.

All traces of his Chinese upbringing, his Chinese wife and his Chinese children had been obliterated by her. Alex Wang was groomed into the perfect English gent, with his suits flown in from Savile Row, his trench coats from Burberry and his shoes from Crockett & Jones. And while his marriage lasted a mere eight years, his love affair with all things English continued to flourish.

Emma and his daughters had moved back to the Home Counties, and now his only interaction with them was the annual visit to their eye-wateringly expensive boarding school. Emma, rather Lady Emma Granger, was firmly ensconced in her country manor, married to a Lord with one foot in the grave. She seemed happy and always welcomed Alex as an old chum. Theirs, at least, had been an amicable divorce.

As he stared out of the reflective floor-to-ceiling windows in his luxury apartment on The Peak, Alex wondered what Hong Kong would have been like if the British had never left. Probably more civilised, he guessed, but no less cut-throat. Now, it was less about your antecedents and the old-boys-network, and more about keeping the rotating door of politicos properly greased, with the right people in the right places happy.

He'd played the game long enough to know that the rules were always changing. The one constant was human greed, whether on full display or hidden behind political rhetoric. Besides, he had enough money to keep the most gluttonous appetites satiated.

As for himself, yes, he enjoyed the many benefits of his wealth, whether that was his extensive property portfolio - a house in Repulse Bay, an apartment in Manhattan, New York, another house in Mayfair, London, and several others he struggled to remember, let alone visit; his custom-made clothes and shoes; his collection of Rolex and Cartier watches; his Caron Poivre perfumes; his stable of Aston Martins, Lamborghinis, Jaguars and Bugattis. Still, at heart he was a simple man with simple wants. The largest of it being the desire for companionship. He wanted a woman by his side. A beautiful woman who was intelligent, compassionate, understanding, incapable of jealousy, and uninterested in reproducing. Surely, with all this wealth at his disposal, that wasn't too much to ask?

His mind stumbled across one of his last conversations with Chiyon, from the night she was packing her suitcase to return to Wong Tai Sin, a district they had both grown up in.

"Alex, you have already found success, but I hope you find happiness too," she'd said, brushing the tears from her eyes as she folded her simple nightshirt in thirds and placed it in her suitcase.

Drunk on his new love, he had sneered at her.

"What makes you think I haven't already?"

That's when she had looked at him with such sadness in her eyes that he had been compelled to drop his own.

"If you ever need me, you know where to find me." She had snapped the case shut and then left the room to pack the children's things.

He had never contacted her after that day, but made sure that she and the children were provided for. Now, he wondered whether she had prophesied his loneliness nearly twenty years ago?

Alex decided at that very moment that he was done with feeling maudlin. He was a man of action, and wallowing was not his style. In the course of his life he had realised that women were replaceable, but good employees were not.

He picked up the phone and rang Joseph Cai, confident that his longest-serving and most loyal employee would still be at work at nearly 10 p.m. Sure enough, the phone was answered within minutes.

"Wang sir?"

"Joseph, I need you to build me something."

Joseph Cai was used to his boss' strange ideas, most of which turned out to be impracticable and had to be binned. But the ones that took off, well, those were the ones that had given Alex Wang the moniker of being a 'visionary'; a man who had brought the future into the present, a man whose many inventions—whether they were sustainable fuel sources, renewable energy, biodegradable batteries or the zero-waste factory initiative—had put him on the cover of Time magazine no less than five times. But what he was asking of him was impossible!

Now, Alex Wang was looking him straight in the eye and asking, "Why can't it be done?"

"Sir, it's one thing to grow organs in the lab..."

"No. It's not one thing, it's an exact thing - an exact science! We created a biologically compatible 3D scaffold containing all the biochemical messages in the correct configuration to trigger the formation of these organs."

"But sir, it took us years to devise the method to modify the naturally occurring biological polymers to trigger chemical adhesion of protein messages to the scaffold."

"And we've mastered it! Don't we provide organs all over the world? Our nearest competitors are still scrambling to decode hydrogel scaffolds with different signals."

Joseph stayed silent for a beat. He knew that arguing with the boss when he was in a mood like this was futile. Then he looked up, his eyes shining.

"Does it have to be entirely human?"

"What do you mean?" Alex looked at him, an eyebrow raised.

"Our BioTech labs have been successfully producing pets for over ten years."

"Joseph, I want a wife, not a cat."

"But what if she was the first HumTech woman we produced? What if you could tweak her as desired? I mean, she would be mostly human and lab-grown of course, but with just enough machinery inside that if we needed we could go in and make changes."

Alex's smile widened.

"There's my genius! Are we going to get into any trouble with the Bioethics people?"

"Only if they find out. Which they won't."

"When can you get started?"

"Straight away. But it could take up to six months to get the proto-type built."

"Then do it. If we crack this, it could be revolutionary!"

"This might get us the Nobel Prize."

"Not so fast, Joseph! We'd have to prove that our intent was purely altruistic."

"Sir, I'm sure you could do anything you put your mind to."

Alex steepled his fingers together and stared at Joseph, a smile playing about his lips.

"Yes, I think I could."

Chiyon had been Alex's childhood sweetheart. From neighbours to friends, then lovers to a married couple, they had navigated the first three decades of their lives together. There was never a time that Alex was without Chiyon, or Chiyon was without Alex. Everyone knew they adored one another.

As a boy, Alex had been curious and incredibly bright, but very few people had believed that Alex could achieve all that he claimed he would. Not even his parents, modest and self-effacing, could understand his ambition, acumen or vision. Only Chiyon understood and supported him, unwaveringly. Love such as that, his mother had told him when he left Chiyon for Emma, came by only once in a life-time, and he had thrown it away for a social-climbing Englishwoman.

Alex did not want to listen. It was obvious why his mother took Chiyon's side. Not only was she her best friend's daughter, but Chiyon also kept him connected to his roots. Now he wanted to soar, and those same roots were holding him back.

Still, he had to acknowledge, if only to himself, that he had never again felt the sort of love that Chiyon had bestowed upon him. A love so strong and so powerful that he had felt cocooned and protected from all the slings and arrows of the world. With Emma, and later with Anastasia, he had taken on the protector's role, and although he never showed it, it chafed his soul.

Now, as he sat at his desk in the WangCo headquarters compiling a list of qualities he wanted in his HumTech wife, he thought back to all that had attracted him to his three wives.

With Chiyon, it was how understanding she was. She had never once questioned his ambition or his methods. She had listened quietly when he spoke, and allowed him the space for his flights of fancy. She had faced the misery of poverty and the suddenness of wealth with equanimity. She had taken care of his parents as if they were her own, and given him two boys, as any good Chinese wife would.

As for Emma, while she had only given him girls, she had been everything that Chiyon couldn't be. She was the elegant companion that he could take to his corporate lunches and dinners. She was witty and sparkling, a conversationalist par excellence with an eye for quality. She had given him the sophisticated veneer that propelled him even higher in the social stratosphere, giving him access to people far removed from the humdrum existence of the hoi polloi. The daughter of a diplomat, her extensive education, expensive tastes, and expansive reach were all the fuel his ambition had needed. She was the right girl for the right moment.

Anastasia was a mistake, and a costly one at that. Steeped in loneliness after his divorce from Emma, he had allowed himself to be seduced by a girl barely out of her teens. Maybe his ego had recognised an ambition and an iron-will as strong as his own. While Anastasia was easily the most beautiful out of his three wives, she was also the hardest, the most materialistic and conniving. But she had been a tigress in bed, giving him the sort of pleasure he had never experienced before or since. With her on his arm, he had finally arrived.

Now, he took out his Tibaldi Fulgor Nocturnus and started making his list. But before he put pen to paper, he considered the exquisite workmanship of the ultra-expensive pen he held in his left hand. Comprising 945 black diamonds that covered the cap and most of the barrel, its design was based on the Divine Proportion of Phi, or the Golden Ratio. That, he decided, would be where his list would begin.

1. A woman conforming to the Golden Ratio. Her face and body perfectly proportioned in the ratio of 1.618

2. Her hair the colour of corn silk, her eyes the green of a marrow, her limbs long and smooth, and her complexion like peaches and cream

3. Her constitution: healthy and robust

4. Her disposition: sanguine

5. Intelligence levels high, but I.Q. no higher than 130

6. Ability to converse, charm, flatter and impress, with none of it being obvious

7. No maternal instincts whatsoever

8. Excellent organisational abilities allowing her to run all the households efficiently, and, if need be, remotely

9. Inability to nag, complain or harangue

10. Most importantly: ability to perform like a gymnast in bed. Not requiring any pleasing in return

He sat back in his chair, satisfied that he had covered everything needed to create the perfect prototype of his ideal wife. If this worked out as he envisioned, he could imagine it revolutionising marriage. Who would need stupid, weepy, grasping, fallible human women when you could have the epitome of sublimity in a lab-grown, machine incorporating, HumTech wife?

The lady shuffling towards her house looked a lot older than her fifty years. Occasionally, she stopped and took a deep breath, holding on to the wall for support. Her lungs were slowly giving up on her, but she refused to accept defeat just yet. In one hand she carried a basket filled with fresh produce: bok choy[1], white radish, eggplant and soybean sprouts. She still cooked for herself daily. Her children had long flown the nest, but whenever they visited, they asked for their favourite dishes, and she enjoyed keeping them happy.

She unlocked the door to her little house. Inside, traces of jasmine incense greeted her, a remainder from her ancestor veneration earlier in the day. Surrounded by the ghosts of her elders, she never felt alone, secure in the knowledge that she was being looked after from the beyond. Someday soon she would be with them, and she would look down benevolently upon her own children and grandchildren.

She stored her vegetables for later use and then sat down in her favourite chair. From that vantage point she eyed her chinoiserie scenery jewellery cabinet that she insisted on keeping in the living room, much to her sons' annoyance. Finished with a hand-painted landscape, the beautiful jewellery cabinet had a mirrored lift-top and felt-lined ring trays. Contained within it were the few pieces of jewellery she had held on to, giving the rest to her daughters-in-law. However, it was the cabinet itself that she prized above all else. It had been a wedding present to her over thirty years ago.

She closed her eyes, remembering the moment her new husband had presented it to her.

"For you, my *Xīngān*."

His heart and liver, he'd called her; one he could not live without, one he had spent three months' wages to buy the precious chinoiserie cabinet for. That was love, and she had once had it.

She sighed deeply before doubling up in pain, her chest racked with a fresh series of coughs. There wasn't much time, and now, she wondered if it was worth reaching out to Alex to say a final goodbye?

"She is beautiful." Alex eyed the sleeping woman, a white sheet covering her body. "How much longer before she's functional?"

"We've grown most of the organs, and her brain really is more of a supercomputer which will store all the information and data required to function optimally. If you need to switch her off for a while, there is a tiny button at the base of her scalp, where the head meets the neck. It's undetectable unless you know what you're looking for. Here, feel for it..." Joseph guided Alex's fingers to it.

"Yes, all that's good, but how much longer?" Alex was impatient now, the six months having stretched into eight.

"Well, Wang sir, we've been having a few issues."

"Such as?"

"The heart. It refuses to grow the way we need it to."

"What do you mean?"

"We've ended up with a five-chambered heart and even a seven-chambered one, but a real, proper heart that won't malfunction is proving to be a challenge."

"How does it matter how many chambers it has, as long as it circulates the blood?"

"Well, I was trying to keep her as human as possible. The alternative is the mechanical heart, which we use in the Techpets. They function as normal hearts, and we have pre-coded the necessary emotions in them. Naturally, the human version will be far superior."

"Then do it." Alex stared out of the small glass panel on the door of the inner laboratory, out into the white nothingness of the corridor, thinking.

"Remember what I told you. I want none of the negative emotions: no jealousy, no anger, no sadness. I want her to be a cheerful companion, one that I'll be glad to return to at the end of a day—not dread what I'm coming home to."

"I completely understand Wang sir." Joseph grinned in complicity.

Alex wondered whether Joseph was married. In the twenty-five years that he had worked for WangCo, Joseph had never mentioned his private life, and Alex had never asked. This arrangement suited them both perfectly, and why fix something that wasn't broken?

"These pets..." Alex wondered aloud, "are the owners satisfied? Do they make good substitutes?"

"We have had no complaints so far, although a few owners switched them off after a few years and got live ones instead."

"Did they say why?"

"Honestly, sir, we didn't ask. As long as they aren't coming back for a refund or replacement, our responsibility ends once the sale is completed."

"But Joseph, aren't you curious why?"

"Wang sir, I have long decided that people, unlike machines, are far harder to decode. I would much rather utilise my time in more productive ways. Besides, we have the retail arm that handles that end of the business."

"Hmm, yes." Alex once again looked at the beautiful prototype on the bed. "And you said that I could shut her off whenever I desired?"

"Yes, shut off, put into sleep mode, send her in for repairs that I would personally oversee - anything you desire, sir."

"I cannot wait to see the finished product then."

"Soon, Wang sir. You will have the perfect wife soon."

She strode through the Yorkshire moors; the wind whipping her hair into a frenzy. In a distance she spied Max and Milo, her Staffordshire bull terriers, running ahead. She whistled to them, but the wind carried her whistle away. Within moments the rain started pelting down, drenching her through her jacket, and she cursed under her breath. Hamish had warned her, but she hadn't listened and now, here she was, caught in a downpour miles away from the house.

Squelching through the mud she called out to the Staffies again, and they came bounding out of nowhere, their tongues lolling as they approached her with inquisitive eyes.

"Okay boys, we'll shelter here for a bit."

She stood under a ramshackle structure, probably a former shed. It was now little more than a few planks of wood that had stayed joined while the rest had fallen away. But it was enough to keep the worst of the rain out. The dogs sat at her feet, panting patiently and waiting for their mistress to give them the signal.

She wiped her face with the sleeve of her Barbour jacket, noticing the smell of mothballs that permeated nearly all her clothes these days. The antique engagement ring Hamish had given her was encrusted with mud from when she'd mucked out the horses earlier. She examined it now. It was a rather beautiful thing; a family heirloom dating back to Queen Victoria. She never took it off her finger. Not so much out of any love for it, but more for what it symbolised - stature and royalty.

But around her neck hung another diamond, a four carat Princess cut, a nearly flawless gem that had once sat on the fourth finger of her left hand. She had broken the ring down, converting the diamond to a pendant that swung from a slim gold chain. She never took that off, either.

First loves are hard to forget, even if they cost you more than you would have initially surmised. Even if they come at the cost of another woman's happiness.

She should never have set her sights on another's husband. Her father had warned her that nothing good would come of it.

"Don't marry that Chinaman, Emma. I don't trust him one bit."

"Papa, you don't trust any man who tries to date your daughter."

"This is different. He's nearly a decade older, and his background... How has he made all this money? Where has he come from? And then, the wife and the children?"

"Firstly, Papa, I'm shocked that you, as a diplomat, would use such racist language! Secondly, he's only seven years older than me. You are fifteen years older than Mummy, so there! And we're in love. His wife and he sort of fell into marriage. It was almost arranged, their families being friends and all that. Come on, Papa, surely you can see he makes me happy? Isn't that enough?"

"How long for, Emma? You know what they say... When a man marries his mistress, he creates a job vacancy..."

"Oh piffle!"

How had she not seen it? In the heady first years of wedded bliss, she had set about making him into the perfect husband. He was already handsome and intelligent, but she had equipped him with finesse and polish. Then he had cheated, and she'd found out. He'd grovelled, and she'd forgiven, only for the entire pattern to be repeated ad nauseam through their time together. Until the last occasion, when she'd walked out on him to marry Hamish, nearly forty years her senior.

Had Papa been around, he'd have mouthed "I told you so." Mummy had been ecstatic to have her daughter and granddaughters return home, no longer having to play the doting mother-in-law to a man she could barely stand.

The rain had turned into a drizzle. She wondered why her mind was fixating so much on Alex these days. She saw him once a year, but had little to do with him otherwise. Her divorce settlement had made her a wealthy woman, and she no longer begrudged Alex his success or his women. Her own girls considered Hamish more of their father than they did the remote man who rarely visited them and spent most of the time on his phone when he did.

Emma sighed deeply. She hoped he was happy after he'd divorced the last bimbo. She wasn't sure what happiness meant anymore, anyway. Creature comforts, or the comfort of being loved unconditionally? She'd tried the latter, but ended up settling for the former.

Tomorrow, she thought to herself as she walked back to the house. Tomorrow she'd call him. If she remembered.

The voice.

"It's not right." Alex frowned.

"But it's exactly what you wanted, like honey sliding over muskmelon."

"It has no character." Alex remembered Emma's dulcet tones, her perfect intonation, and the way each of her sentences ended on a lilt.

"I'll send you a recording. Listen to it and program that into her."

"Yes, Wang sir." Joseph looked sheepish. "There is something else…"

"Yes?"

"A few of the other scientists have started asking questions."

"They have all signed non-disclosures, haven't they?"

"Yes, but this project has taken up so much time, and they are wondering what we are really making now…"

"Their job isn't to wonder, it's to work, and work as per my specifications!"

"They keep saying that we are making a monster in here!"

"What kind of idiots have you hired, Cai? These are meant to be scientists, not teenage girls with fevered imaginations!"

"Maybe if we let them see her then we could put all the rumours to rest…"

"No! Absolutely not! If they think we are creating Frankenstein's monster in here, then let them. I'm more than willing to let them go. Let's see if they can find a job that pays them as well as this one."

"It's just that as scientists it is in their nature to question and probe, and so far they have only developed components; factory parts that are being assembled remotely and in secrecy. They have no idea of the whole that they are contributing towards."

"I'm not here to allay their curiosity, nor are you. Now, take me in to see her."

Joseph led the way through the winding white corridors of the laboratory, stopping at multiple doors and using the access pass that only he possessed. Alex had a copy in the safe in his office, but he didn't envision using it. It was only a matter of weeks before she was ready, and between Joseph and him, they would smuggle her out at night, when no one else was around.

She was sitting up in a chair, wearing a thin slip that just about covered her. Her eyes flicked to them as they walked in, but conveyed no expression.

"Has she been activated yet?"

"No, Wang sir. I'm just checking her motor skills at the moment, but once I've done the final tweaks, we'll do a trial run here. If, after that, she is to your satisfaction, then you can take her home with you."

"Can I touch her?"

"She's all yours, sir. You can do what you like."

Joseph moved back, allowing Alex to reach out and touch the HumTech P18K.

"Will you leave us alone for a while?"

Joseph exited the room wordlessly.

Alex moved towards the woman, his fingers touching her hair (soft, shiny), her face (beautiful), trailing down her neck and over her collarbone, moving aside the slip to reach down and touch her breasts. She remained motionless, her breath even and shallow, watching him with a disembodied interest. Alex felt himself harden. Yes, this was good. Very, very good. She turned him on, and that was even before she had been programmed to perform for him. Anticipation tingled in his body. He couldn't wait to bed his creation.

Power. That was what had first attracted her to him. Power was a potent aphrodisiac. As a young girl, she had felt powerless in a home governed by the iron fist of a violent father and brothers who had followed suit. She had little but her youth and good looks to trade, but it had been enough.

That close to the nerve centre of power and money, her own tastes had become expensive. Although, in her mind, she more than paid her way.

She was a performer. A nun one day, a schoolgirl the next - nothing was too outlandish or too extreme for her. After all, she had traded her body for a lavish life, and if the payment was role-play and stunts in the bedroom, it was fair enough.

Love had never even entered the equation. Alex was more than twice her age when she met and seduced him. He was already balding and paunchy, but in him she saw a sort of protector. A father figure who wouldn't hit her one minute and rape her the next.

But what Alex did to her was much, much worse. He denied her the one thing she had craved her whole life.

She had gone to him for the first time, barely two months after their lavish seaside wedding.

"*Zaichik...*" She'd sidled up to him while he read the news on his latest tablet computer, knowing he loved being called a bunny. "I have some news."

"Hmmm?" He'd barely looked up.

"I'm pregnant."

Then he had looked up, and his eyes had been as cold as the ice shavings he liked in his *kakigori*[2] cocktails.

"Abort it."

"But..."

"Go to Dr Huan, he'll take care of it."

There had never been any discussion, any consideration of what she might have wanted. All her life Anastasia had dreamt of being a mother, of showering her children with the love and affection that she had been denied. Motherhood had been her one abiding ambition, the only truly worthwhile job that a woman could do.

When that was snatched from her not once or twice, but multiple times, her heart grew hard with hatred. She used his money like toilet paper, throwing it away on fripperies and extravagances that he barely blinked an eyelid at. She changed her appearance so often that her own image in the mirror caught her by surprise. She had her breasts enlarged to disproportionate levels; the fat sucked out of her thighs and placed in her butt cheeks, weekly bee venom facials that made her skin glow, fillers that gave her a perpetual pout.

She became the Barbie doll on his arm. The one that the paparazzi couldn't get enough of, her every move followed, photographed and discussed on the major social media platforms and e-zines of the day.

Anastasia had no female friends. They either hated her or were intimidated by her. As for Alex, he had no real friends either, except for the creepy Joseph Cai who followed him around like a lapdog. When the loneliness and hurt finally overflowed into a public meltdown, Alex Wang cut her out of his life like the diseased limb that she had become.

She was in his house, his perfect woman. Beautiful, serene, and composed, she was neither impressed, nor fazed by his stunning apartment or its incomparable views. Why would she be? She had no yardstick for comparison. She had been birthed into privilege. He was her father, her husband, her mentor, and her world.

"Welcome to your new home, Galatea." He led her into the living room, his hand on her waist, her skin warm and soft, her movements as supple as a ballerina's.

"Galatea? What kind of name is that?" Alex had asked Joseph the night before. Shortly after they had run the tests, Joseph had informed him that he had already named her.

Alex had been irritated by this, wanting to put his own stamp on her; wanting to call her Alexandra after himself. But when Joseph had explained the ancient Greek myth of Pygmalion—the sculptor who fell in love with his creation, Galatea, and how this beautiful statue was brought to life by none other than the goddess Aphrodite who united the couple in marriage—Alex had been appeased and impressed. The name resonated with him deeply.

Now, he looked at his own creation come to life and marvelled at her perfection.

"Would you like to eat something, darling?"

"Only if you wish to, sir."

"No, no. I am not 'sir', I am Alex. Please, call me by my name."

"Yes, Alex." She turned and smiled at him, her eyes as green as the Mediterranean Sea and just as unfathomable.

Overcome, he grabbed her, planting a deep kiss on her lips, plunging his tongue into her mouth, tasting her new and unusual flavours. She responded enthusiastically, her hands moving over his body in a skilful choreography until he no longer remembered where he was and who he was with.

This was bliss. And he deserved every bit of it.

They had gathered together on the rooftop of his penthouse apartment on The Peak to watch Alex Wang marry the mysterious beauty he had started dating only a few short months ago.

No paparazzi were allowed at this small and intimate wedding. Even the guests' mobile phones had been gently confiscated before they entered the premises.

"But who is she? And where has she come from?"

Guests muttered to each other in undertones.

"How old is she? Surely young enough to be his daughter?"

"Look at him. He's glowing. Whatever she's doing to him, it seems to be ageing him in reverse."

"Ah, that's what good sex does, my friend."

"Oh, shut up! They're in love. Look at the way they are with each other. I have never seen Alex this possessive of any of his wives."

"Listen, keep your rumours and innuendos to yourself. We are lucky enough to be invited. I want to stay in Mr Wang's good graces."

Anastasia topped up her glass with the bottle of vintage Dom Perignon that the waiter had left in the ice bucket for her sole use. She still wasn't sure why Alex had invited her to the wedding. Was it to rub her nose in it? To show off his perfect, beautiful young bride? She had been young and beautiful too, once, a long time ago. Wait until this one found out that Mr Alex Wang had no soul.

"Hello Anastasia," a soft voice spoke at her shoulder. She nearly jumped out of her skin, splashing a bit of champagne out of her flute as she turned to face her nemesis.

"Emma," she breathed, shock making her voice hoarse.

"Never thought we'd be in the same room ever again, did you?"

Anastasia shook her head, speechless. Emma had always made her dislike evident. Today, however, she seemed almost friendly.

"Don't worry, I won't bite. I got over Alex a long time ago. Anyway, being married to him was no cakewalk, as I'm sure you discovered too. But look at him! He's landed another gorgeous young thing. I suppose they just gravitate towards him because of his wealth..."

"... and power." Anastasia finished the sentence for Emma.

"Yes, that." Emma looked at the couple being congratulated by yet another billionaire and frowned. "Why did he call us to the wedding? I don't know a single soul here, except for you and that strange man... Choi, Chai?"

"Cai. Joseph Cai."

"Yes, him." She set her gin and tonic on the counter behind her and looked around at the fifty-odd people congregating on the rooftop. Where was she? Why hadn't he invited her?

Anastasia watched her with knowing eyes.

"I believe she is sick. Extremely sick. She couldn't make the journey."

"Oh." The breath left Emma's body in a sharp exhale. She had been half-anticipating and half-dreading meeting Chiyon here. Nearly twenty years later, the guilt still gnawed at her insides. She straightened up and looked at Anastasia.

"Well, let's get this over and done with, shall we?"

"What do you mean?"

"Let's go and wish the happy couple. He wants us to. That's why we're here, aren't we?"

"Yes, okay. Let's do it."

If Alex was surprised to see them walk up to him arm in arm, he didn't betray it.

"Hello girls!" He greeted them effusively, planting a kiss on each of their cheeks, welcoming them as though they were his good old friends, not hard-done-by ex-wives. "Meet Galatea."

Emma was first to stretch out her hand. Galatea shook it delicately, smiling politely.

"Congratulations Alex. She is even more beautiful close-up."

"Thank you," Galatea murmured. "But look at how stunning the two of you are. Such a hard act to follow."

"Well," Anastasia said, flattered, "she is nice as well. You better take care of this one, Alex."

"Oh, I intend to!" He guffawed, turning away from them to speak to another guest, pulling Galatea away too.

Later, as they sat nursing their drinks at a bar nearby, Emma said, "I really wanted to talk to her. Notice how he let no one get close to her?"

"Emma," Anastasia said, with a faraway look in her eyes, "something about her reminded me of you. I just can't put my finger on it."

"Come to think of it," Emma answered slowly, "I thought she looked a lot like you, when you were younger."

"It's the voice!" Anastasia sat up, excited. "She sounded just like you!"

"Really? Come on. This is us probably making it all up, thinking we still matter to him. Next, we'll be wondering which part of Chiyon does she resemble?"

"Does she?"

"Nah!"

They shook their heads and laughed together. It was the last time they would ever meet, but they intended to make a night of it.

The wailing had reached a crescendo when Alex walked into the little house he had last been in over thirty years ago. Chiyon's casket was a simple affair, much like the woman herself. She looked peaceful dressed in blue, a colour that had always suited her. Joss sticks were burning around the casket to ensure that she had a safe journey to the netherworld. A large photograph of her sat at the head of the casket, surrounded by wreaths and flowers.

He had brought a bouquet of large white calla lilies. As he placed them at the foot of the casket, a young man came over and held out a cloth band. Alex nodded and let him pin it to his right sleeve. He wondered if the young man was his son, but didn't ask.

The professional mourners kept up their wailing while other members of the family huddled together and wept quietly. Chiyon had been loved by all.

Alex backed away, unable to stand there a moment longer. Why had he come? What good would it do? She was gone, and it was too late to say sorry.

Back in his office, he toyed with the pencil on his desk, his thoughts scattering in a million directions. The news of Chiyon's death had hit him much harder than he had expected it to. There was a finality to it. It was a full stop that allowed no amendments.

Then he thought of the beautiful young woman who waited for him at home, and his pulse quickened. She was everything he had hoped for. Erudite, accomplished, sensual, understanding. Her brain comprehended his every need and supplied him with the very response he needed.

That she never complained, never asked his whereabouts, never felt lonely and was pleased to see him night or day, was just the icing on the cake.

It had been four months since their wedding, and although he had taken Galatea with him everywhere, he had rarely allowed anyone any one-on-one time with her. He wanted to give her this time to learn and adapt to her surroundings. She was soaking all the information up like a sponge; that supercomputer of a brain processing it all and often supplying him with the details his own brain had either forgotten or overlooked. Yes, she would be a formidable asset to him in the times to come.

Tired as he was from the emotions that Chiyon's death had

churned up in him, he couldn't wait to get home to his new bride. In her, every one of his dreams had been realised.

"W... water..." He croaked, his body bathed in sweat. It had been three days, and the fever hadn't broken. His mouth felt like parchment paper and his hands trembled, unable to perform the most basic of tasks.

"It is by the bedside, Alex." Galatea sat on the chair, observing him; smile at the ready.

"P... please..."

She looked at him, cocking her head to one side.

"I don't understand, Alex."

"W... water..." His energy depleted, he fell back on to the pillow. Was she torturing him deliberately? Was she capable of it?

He closed his eyes and thought back over the past year. When had the disenchantment set in? One day, he was deeply and madly in love with her. The next day he couldn't stand the sight of her.

Joseph had programmed her to peak efficiency and as per Alex's own list of requirements. But now, he could see how short sighted that list had really been.

Galatea's constant cheeriness irritated him. Her ready-to-please attitude grated on his nerves. Her acrobatics in the bedroom tired him out. But most of all, her intelligence scared him.

Just the other day he had come home to see her staring at the refrigerator door. Not sure what she was up to, he had waited and watched. As the door had swung open to an unspoken command, his face had paled. She was talking to the gadgets now, as if assembling a machine-army ready to do her bidding.

Was he turning paranoid?

Worst of all, it was he who had created her - this hybrid of human and technology. This being crafted solely for his pleasure, devoid of human foibles and worse still, incapable of any empathy.

His illness had come upon him suddenly, and because he didn't want the shareholders worrying, he'd told Galatea to inform everyone that they were going on a mini-break to one of their private islands. In actual fact, he'd stayed home in bed, delirious with fever. Galatea did his bidding without question, but his incoherent ramblings had been difficult for her to decipher. So, a mound of medicines had piled up on the bedside table, with several glasses of water, just out of his reach.

To her credit, Galatea hadn't budged from his side during his illness, not requiring food or sleep to function. But she had done very little to help him out. She was either incapable or unwilling to take the initiative. And he was too tired and confused to give her clear instructions.

How many days had he lain here? What was wrong with him? What did he really want? Questions circled in his mind like large birds of prey. Whom could he call? Whom did he trust?

"J... Joseph..." He whispered. "Call Joseph."

Then he fell into another fugue state, his body thrashing about in bed while his mind alighted upon a distant shore.

"Wang sir, Wang sir..." Joseph's voice penetrated through the fog in his mind. His eyes opened slowly, everything in his vision blurring and reassembling. Joseph stood in front of him, holding a glass of water. He sat on the bed and put the water to Alex's lips. Alex drank deeply, gulping down the liquid as though it was nectar from the gods.

"T... Thank you Joseph."

"Wang sir, you need a doctor."

"N... no, no doctors. I just need to rest. I will recover soon. But you need to get rid of her." His eyes flickered towards Galatea, who stood behind Joseph, ever smiling, ever compliant.

"Get rid of her?"

"Shut her off, put her to sleep. Whatever you need to do."

"But, but why? I built her exactly how you wanted. If it's repairs she needs..."

"No repairs!" A spasm of pain overtook Alex, and he gasped, clutching Joseph's hand. "P... please. I just... no more... can't take it..."

Joseph shook his hand off and stood up.

"No, Wang sir."

"W... what?"

"I won't do it."

Alex noticed the look that passed between them.

Love.

She had never been Alex's creation. She had been Joseph's. He was the Pygmalion to her Galatea, the creator of this stunning creation. Where Alex had merely fantasised about her, Joseph had built her - painstakingly, limb by limb, growing one organ after another, getting the machine parts of her to talk to the human parts. At which point had he fallen in love? And just what was he willing to do for this love?

"J... Joseph, listen to me," Alex gasped. "She is incapable of love. She is a machine. You will never find happiness with her..."

"But Wang sir, you never found happiness with any of your human wives either."

Alex absorbed the import of his words. Chiyon's face flashed into his mind. Chiyon with all her love, her kindness, her shyness. If he hadn't been able to find happiness with her, what hope had there been of finding it with Emma or Anastasia?

But he had to warn Joseph! He couldn't let him make the same mistake.

Alex tried sitting up in bed, but his head swam with the effort and he fell back upon his pillow.

"Joseph, this, whatever you're feeling for her, it... it isn't real... And it will never be reciprocated... remember, she has no heart..."

Joseph held out his hand to Galatea, who accepted it, smiling at him just as she used to smile at Alex.

"Wang sir, I programmed Galatea to your specifications, but somewhere within her, she always belonged to me. It was only a matter of time before you both realised it."

He looked down at Alex, pity in his eyes.

"She may be part machine, but she is also part human. Those parts I grew and nurtured, much as a mother would. If you considered yourself her father and co-creator, remember, she wouldn't exist if it weren't for me. Now that you are dying, yes, dying, hear this from me. Galatea is mine. And all of this, your empire, that's mine too. You see, your will was altered to leave everything to your beautiful new bride, who will in time marry her husband's best friend and trusted employee."

"You're a fool Joseph!" Alex gasped. "She belongs to nobody. You haven't seen what I..."

His breaths were getting shallower now, his tenuous grasp on life slipping. Thoughts were a jumble, and his body felt like a cage in which his soul flapped its wings, ready to escape. Suddenly, nothing mattered except moving towards that brilliant light that shone in the distance. He felt himself getting lighter, lighter than air, and levitating out of his body. A faint fragrance of jasmine incense wafted into the room. A familiar face smiled kindly at him, holding out her hand, and Alex breathed his last.

Joseph Cai led his Galatea out of the room where his former boss' body lay twisted and spent.

Tomorrow, he would reprogram her to his own specs. Today, he would enjoy her as she was.

~

7

LALA LAKSHMI

Lakshmi Chand had once been a handsome man. However, the athletic build and full head of hair that he had sported in his youth were no longer in his providence. The years had not treated him kindly. Each decade had added rolls of fat to his torso and subtracted the hair off his head. His eyes bulged ever so slightly and the two angry parentheses etched between his eyebrows had been joined by dark patches on his cheeks. A triple chin and a nearly invisible neck that disappeared into a beefy torso gave him the appearance of a large, sullen bullfrog.

Dressed in a white *kurta* [1] pyjama, he sat at his *halwai* [2] shop daily, overseeing the business started eighty years ago by his grandfather, the late great Popat Chand.

He was a taskmaster and all his employees lived in constant fear of being caught in a moment of inefficiency or laziness, and being fired as a result. It wasn't as though other jobs were scarce, but Popat Chand Mithaiwala was the largest and busiest *halwai* shop in the area, and they were paid well by industry standards. However, Lakshmi Chand made sure he extracted his pound of flesh, working them harder and later than any of his rivals would dare to.

Diwali was a few days away, and the two-storey shop was buzzing with customers all day long. This was the most profitable time of the year, and Lakshmi Chand had ordered all his employees to come in earlier than usual. No one was allowed to take leave, no matter what the reason or excuse. Lakshmi Chand, true to his name, intended to bring in as much money (lakshmi) as the festive period would allow.

The *mithai* [3]was prepared two miles away in a small workhouse-cum-factory. Day after day, the *halwais* toiled in its hot and sweaty environment; grinding, kneading, mixing, and frying the sweetmeats enjoyed by the clientele that frequented the glitzy and thoroughly modernised Popat Chand Mithaiwala. Unlike the factory that remained unseen, the shop itself boasted marble floors, chrome fittings and an enormous bronze statue of the *Devi* [4]of wealth and prosperity, *Maa*[5] Lakshmi herself.

Every morning at 9 a.m. Lakshmi Chand prostrated himself in front of the bronze idol of the goddess, offering her the choicest of his sweetmeats and praying for his continued prosperity. The goddess seemed to smile down on him benignly.

Lakshmi Chand wasn't entirely unaware of the aptness of being named after the *devi*, for he had lived up to the moniker in more ways than one. It was he who had brought the old *mithai* shop into the new century by modernising and refurbishing it. It was because of him that the sweets were made to the highest standard and their fame had spread far and wide in the city of Delhi. It was also he who had had the foresight to expand his business beyond just *mithais*, adding to the premises a restaurant that served hot and tasty Indian fast food like *poori aloo*[6], *chhole kulche*[7], *papdi chaat*,[8] *samosas, bhelpuri*[9], *pau bhaji*[10] and other such savoury delights.

Not a fan of sweets himself, it was the savoury food that he gorged on day after day, increasing his girth slowly but surely.

He sat on his perch behind the counter, munching on the first of his many *pakoras* [11]of the day. The *karela* [12]*pakoras* were prepared especially for him as he was the only one who enjoyed the bitterness of the gourd, deep fried in batter and drizzled over by a hot green chilli coriander chutney. He had heard whispers that his employees called him a fat, old bitter gourd, but that didn't bother him a jot. In fact, he rather relished being seen as an authoritarian; a distant and formidable figure. That alone was enough to keep them on the straight and narrow.

As he licked the crumbs off his fingers, seemingly oblivious to the surrounding hubbub, his mind was sharply focussed on the business at hand. Diwali was only four days away, and he had temporarily closed down the restaurant side of the business to house the many boxes of sweets that would be required to satisfy his hungry customers. The suppliers he had been using for several years had suddenly hiked up their prices for the beautifully decorated cardboard boxes that housed the *mithai* from Popat Chand Mithaiwala. Their distinctive purple and pink *bandhani* [13]print covers were the signature aesthetic of his store. He had no intention of paying them the extra money, but just as canny, they had held out on the difference and not sent him the last consignment of 5000 boxes. The situation had reached an impasse. Lakshmi Chand knew that he was at a disadvantage because he needed the boxes, but he also knew that none of his competitors would buy them for fear of their products being confused with his brand.

Slowly and with great delicacy, he put aside his plate and let out a big belch.

"Bring me the phone," he snarled at Raju, his second-in-command. The slight, anxious young man rushed to do his *sahib*'s bidding. He brought over the old red rotary-style phone and set it down in front of Lala Lakshmi, still marvelling inwardly at the fact that the Lala refused to own a mobile phone.

"Number *laga!*" [14] the Lala instructed, rattling off a phone number from memory. Raju dialled hastily, his fingers trembling ever so slightly as he waited for the dial to rotate back noisily to its place after every '9' (the last number on the rotary face) was dialled. The line connected, and he handed the phone over to the Lala.

"*Haan* [15] Shastri, Lala Lakshmi here. Yes, yes, I am okay. Now listen to me. You remember that print I had given to you a few years ago? Yes, I want 5000 boxes made with the same print on the cover. Purple and pink, and 'Popat Chand Mithaiwala' embossed in gold.

Yes." He listened for a bit. "I want them done by this evening and delivered to the store. I don't care how late it is, I will be here and so will Raju. Don't worry, you will get the payment in cash. I want to teach those *chutiyas* [16]a lesson. They think they can blackmail me? Ha!"

Handing the receiver back to Raju, Lala Lakshmi fairly gloated with glee. "I did not get to where I am by being taken for a fool. Raju, call Hari & Co. and tell them the order is cancelled."

"But Lalaji, they've already made the boxes. In fact, I just had a message from Hariji that delivery could be made today upon the balance being paid off. What will they do with all those boxes?"

"Raju! Do you work for them or for me, huh? Hari can take the boxes and throw them in the Yamuna river for all I care. He thought he could outsmart me! Now he can think again."

"But Lalaji, your family's association with them goes back to your grandfather's days. They have always supplied our boxes. We don't even know if the new suppliers will have the same quality or not."

"But, but, but... Is that all you can say? If Hari wants our business, he will have to lower his prices now. Otherwise, there are many other suppliers willing to take business from Popat Chand Mithaiwala. As far as family association goes, there is no room for sentiment in business. If he can hike his prices last minute, I can take my business elsewhere too. Now, go and see what those useless workers are up to."

He watched Raju rush off and sat back in his chair, a small satisfied smile playing about his lips. Nothing brought him more happiness than the use of his wits.

Truth was that Lala Lakshmi was bored. The business was thriving, and although he sat in the store daily, he knew that all of it could run like a well-oiled machine even in his absence. He had hired and trained Raju for this very purpose. But what was he supposed to do with his time?

He had not taken a vacation in over a decade. The last time he had left the shop for an extended period was when he'd gone to

Benares to immerse his father's ashes in the Ganges. He supposed that didn't really count as a vacation. Mala, his sister, kept inviting him to Lucknow where she had settled with her schoolteacher husband and their three children, but the very thought of being in a bustling family environment made his stomach turn. No, his place was right here, at the helm of his business. This would be where he'd live and die, eating his *karela pakoras* and doing his daily Sudoku.

All day long people entered and exited the store through its glass front doors. Lala Lakshmi watched the parade of customers, hawk-eyed as always. It never failed to amuse him to see how the women worked around their menfolk stealthily, agreeing at first to their demands, then slowly turning them towards the sweets they'd really wanted to purchase; often the more expensive products. He'd trained his salesmen to fawn over and flatter the women's choices, telling them just how clever they were to select the best sweetmeats on offer. This didn't just ensure a hefty bill, but also repeat customers year after year.

Diwali was his favourite time of the year. It was his most profitable, no doubt, but it was also to do with the change in the weather; the hot and muggy days giving way to cooler evenings. The way the women dressed in their festive and colourful silk saris and *salwar kameezes*[17]. Houses were cleaned and painted, with *rangoli* [18]decorations made in front of their doorways. Everyone seemed relaxed and happy, as though waiting for *Devi Maa* Lakshmi to come and bestow her blessings for the new year.

Years ago in school, he'd had to study Tulsidas' *Ramcharitmanas*, the long epic poem about Lord Rama's victory over evil. Little had registered except for the fourteen-year banishment that the heir to the throne had accepted from his father and scheming stepmother, and that during the exile his wife, Sita, had been kidnapped by the demon king Ravana. The beauty of the poetry was entirely lost on his sensibilities. But Rama's return as the rightful heir to the throne after reclaiming his wife was legend and lore known to every Indian. It was this that was celebrated year after year throughout India. A victory of good over evil and the importance of letting our inner light shine in the darkest of circumstances.

Lala Lakshmi didn't much care for any of the spiritual lessons within the text. He was much too old and cynical to believe that there was anything beyond this life. One had to make the best of what one was given. And seeing that he had been given a business, he'd made the best of that.

As for his own youthful ambitions, he didn't dwell upon those much. What good would an MBA have done a *halwai* like him, anyway? He'd used whatever business acumen he had without needing to get a degree to prove how smart he was. So what if it would have meant living in America for a few years? Having independence, living as a normal student with no responsibilities — these were all just exaggerated dreams sold to naïve youngsters, as his father had pointed out. Lala Gopi Chand had visited America as a tourist once and not liked it one bit. Too big, too soulless. He didn't think his son would like it either. Indians belonged in India. Lakshmi Chand had never even formulated a rebuttal in his head.

A waft of perfume made him look up from his books. Two ladies had just walked into the store and stood with their back to the counter, looking at the *barfis*[19] on display at the opposite counter. One was short and shrill as she pointed out the various flavours. But it was the other one who caught and held his attention. There was something familiar about the curve of her back, the way she tossed her hair, her sinuous movements.

She was dressed in a simple cream *churidaar kameez*[20] and had a heavily embellished green and gold *dupatta*[21] thrown over her shoulders. The *kurta* had a peephole back knotted together with two strings, lending a certain sensuousness to the simple outfit. It was like a white peacock had walked into a sea of geese.

"I think you should stick to the classic *kaju katli*,[22] Nam. You can't go wrong with that."

He strained to listen to her answer, every nerve end prickling. Her low voice was just as soft and delicate as he remembered. Like little silver bells.

Nam.

Namita.

A rush of memories engulfed him, even as she turned to face the counter he sat at. He shrank back, trying to hide behind his employees.

Sunglasses were perched on her head, and her auburn locks tumbled down to her waist. Her fingernails were painted a soft baby pink, and a huge solitaire glittered on the fourth finger of her left hand.

She moved towards the glass display, and once again, a waft of some exotic perfume reached him.

"I was thinking of getting some *rasogollas* [23] too. The children like them. And Raj likes the *sohan halwa*[24]."

"He must need a hammer to break that! I nearly chipped a tooth last year and swore to myself I'd never buy it again." Her friend kept talking while Namita examined the sweets behind the glass.

"There really is quite a selection here, Poonam. I'm very impressed."

"Nam, I told you I was taking you to the best *halwai* shop in Delhi. Did you think I was lying?"

He examined her face covertly. Twenty-five years had wrought a few changes. She had crow's feet near her eyes, and her mouth drooped ever so slightly at the corners. Her jawline wasn't quite what it used to be, and grey roots were showing in her auburn mane. But none of that mattered, because, to him, she seemed to have grown even more beautiful.

There was a part of him that wanted to call out to her, to ask her how she was. To ask her if she was happy, if America was treating her well, and whether she thought of him at all. Another part just wanted to shrink away; disappear into the background so she would not see him as he was now. That she would always remember him as young, virile and handsome. A man she had once thought she might marry.

Suddenly she looked up and caught his eye. Then she pointed with her index finger at the *sohan halwa*.

"Do you only do this by the kilo? Can I just buy one piece?" Turning to her friend she said, "Raj is so careful about his weight that he'll get annoyed if I buy more than that for him."

She looked back at him, waiting for a response. Unable to speak, he nodded mutely.

"Okay, thank you. Can you pack up half a kilo of the *kaju katli*, one kilo of the *rasogollas*, and one piece of the *sohan halwa*? How much does it come to?"

Thankfully, one of the other employees took over. Lala Lakshmi retreated to his corner, shaken. She hadn't recognised him! Not even a flicker!

He watched her make the payment and leave the store. His heart pounded as he watched the only woman he had ever loved walk away from him again.

With shaky steps, he went up the stairs to the toilet he kept reserved for himself. Looking at his face in the mirror, he tried to see what she had seen. A fat, balding man looked back at him. With a thud he sat down on the commode, his heart beating peculiarly. When had life passed him by?

Half an hour later, having composed himself, he returned to the counter. That was another lifetime ago. This was today. The here and now. And he'd be damned if he was going to let a spectre from the past affect him in any way.

Raju came up to him, his thin frame humming with anxiety.

"Lala*ji*, can one of the other employees stay with you tonight? It's just that my wife called a few minutes ago. Our daughter isn't well, and she wants me to take her to the doctor."

"What is wrong with her?"

"She has had a fever since this morning, and my wife is getting worried because she's not getting any better."

"So tell her to give her some Crocin."

"She has, Lalaji. But just to be sure it's nothing else, she wants me to take her to the doctor."

"Can't she take her?"

"But I am the one with the scooter."

Irritated, Lala Lakshmi looked at his loyal employee.

"Well, I can't spare you this evening, so you'll just have to make alternate arrangements."

For a moment it seemed that Raju would argue with him, and Lala Lakshmi couldn't wait to give him a tongue lashing. Instead, he bowed his head sorrowfully and walked away.

The day's business was over. The store's doors had been shut at 9 p.m. Lala Lakshmi and Raju sat together in the back of the strangely quiet store waiting for Shastri's men to deliver the boxes.

Each man was lost in his own thoughts. Lala Lakshmi once again thought of Namita, and how well she had looked. She'd seemed happy, as though everything in life had come up roses. But then she'd always been a lucky one. Had he really expected her to wilt with suffering? Would that have gladdened his heart more?

Near 10 p.m. one of Shastri's men knocked on the door. The lorry was unloaded and the boxes brought into the storeroom, from where they'd be transferred to the workshop tomorrow. Raju counted and inspected them while Lala Lakshmi brought out the agreed sum of money. When each party was satisfied, Shastri's men left in the lorry. Then Raju and Lala Lakshmi locked up after themselves.

Raju walked with Lala Lakshmi to the car, making sure that the sahib was okay before going to his scooter to head home to his wife and sick daughter.

Lakshmi Chand turned the key in the ignition, but the car refused to start. He tried again and again, but nothing worked. Raju was rounding the corner when he heard his boss' voice calling out.

"*Ey* Raju, the car is not working. You'll have to drop me home on your scooter."

Raju looked at his boss, and his face blanched. He had no choice, so once again he complied. When Lala Lakshmi climbed on to the pillion seat, the entire back end of the scooter sank lower. Raju calculated that he wouldn't be home before midnight at this rate, as Lalaji lived in the opposite direction to him. And he had to start at 7 a.m. the next morning to ensure the boxes were transferred to the workhouse. Biting back a yawn, he drove Lalaji home.

Lakshmi Chand hadn't ridden pillion in years. He wouldn't have admitted it to anyone, but he was quite enjoying it. The chilly breeze ruffled the few strands of hair on his head, the night sky seemed filled with stars that twinkled brighter than he'd noticed lately, and as Raju weaved his way through the night traffic, Lala Lakshmi had a sudden vision of himself as a teenager, riding a motorcycle like Amitabh Bachchan in some '80s Bollywood movie. He sighed with a quiet happiness. Maybe all he needed to do was get rid of the Mercedes and get a Bajaj scooter.

When Raju dropped him off in front of his palatial home, Lala Lakshmi barely acknowledged the favour, waving him off with a gruff "don't be late tomorrow."

The chowkidar saluted him as he came in. The maid rubbed the sleep out of her eyes as she opened the door, asking if the sahib was hungry. He dismissed her, ambling towards the liquor chest. There he poured himself a stiff peg of Johnnie Walker Blue and sat on the old rocking chair that had once belonged to his grandfather.

It was there that he woke up at 2 a.m.; whisky glass empty on the floor, his stomach growling in hunger. Groaning, he pulled himself out of the chair and made his way to the kitchen. Opening the refrigerator, he looked for something to eat. The maid had cooked *daal*[25], *bhindi*[26] and rice, but he couldn't be bothered to heat things up. So he rooted around some more before finding sliced cheese in a packet. He took a couple of slices and a carton of orange juice, struggling to hold it all as he shut the refrigerator door with his knee.

He turned to look for a glass and a shrill scream escaped him.

Lala Popat Chand, his late great and deceased grandfather, stood in front of him looking distinctly unhappy.

The cheese and orange juice carton slipped out of his hands as he struggled to comprehend what he was seeing. Trembling, he reached forward to touch his grandfather, but his hand passed through thin air. Horrified, he backed away, then turned on his heel and ran to his room, locking the door behind him.

His heart thudding, he listened for noises behind the door but heard nothing. Chanting the *Gayatri Mantra*, a prayer he remembered warding off his childhood terrors, Lala Lakshmi went into the bathroom and splashed his face with cold water.

Had he been dreaming? Was it some kind of hallucination - a combination of stress, alcohol and poor diet? He vowed to himself that he'd have a health check after Diwali. Having calmed down, he changed into his pyjamas and re-entered the bedroom.

Lala Popat Chand sat cross-legged on the bed, waiting patiently for him. Dressed in his usual *khadi*[27] jacket over a white *kurta* pyjama, with a Gandhi *topi* on his head, he looked no older than the eighty-four years he'd perished at.

Lakshmi Chand's legs buckled, and he felt himself falling in slow motion. His grandfather observed him impassively.

"D...*dadaji*[28]?" Lala Lakshmi's voice came out in a tremulous whisper.

"Who else?" His grandfather countered.

"B...but you're dead..."

"I thought so too. Then I was rudely despatched here to give you a message."

"A m...message? W...what kind of message?"

"Get up off the floor, you oaf. *Buddhu*[29]! I can't have you sitting there like an idiot gawping at me. Look at the state you're in!"

"B...but... but..."

"What 'but but'? I'm in a hurry here. So sit on the bed next to me. I want to give you the message and be on my way again."

"On your way?" Lala Lakshmi hauled himself up off the floor with difficulty and tentatively perched himself next to the ghostly figure of his grandfather, who looked even more disgruntled now than he ever had in his lifetime. "Where are you going?"

"You'll find out in your own good time. Now, listen carefully. Someone will visit you tonight. Make sure you give her a good welcome, not like the one you just gave me."

Lala Lakshmi shivered. "Another ghost?"

"Just shut up and listen. This is a VIP, okay? You treat her right. She's taken you on as a special case, although I can't imagine why."

"Who is she?"

"I have to go now. Before I leave, I must tell you just what I think of everything that you have done to my legacy..."

Lala Lakshmi forgot his fear, leaning forward to receive the first words of praise he was ever going to get from his grandfather. But just like a television connection gone bad, his grandfather's image folded upon itself, words garbled, and in a few static bursts he disappeared entirely.

Lakshmi Chand rubbed his eyes and looked around the room. Everything looked exactly the same. The bedcover was still a royal blue, the curtains the same colour with a pale blue embroidered pattern upon them. In the corner sat a large LCD television, hardly ever used. His jackets hung behind the door, still in the plastic covers the dry cleaners had returned them in. His *Kolhapuri chappals*[30] sat next to the Italian suede shoes he'd bought on a whim and never worn. An old black-and-white photograph of his parents sat on his bedside table. The night light the maid had put on flickered slightly.

Looking around him once again, he shook his head and pinched himself hard. Owww, he swore under his breath; that hurt! So he was not asleep. Then it must have been the whisky. What else could have produced a hallucination that vivid? He'd get rid of the damn bottle first thing tomorrow morning. Even though it had been bloody expensive. But no, first thing tomorrow, he'd throw it in the bin.

He lay down on his back, pulling the covers up to his chin, and fell into a deep, dreamless sleep almost immediately.

. . .

It seemed only minutes later that he felt a feather-light touch on his arm. He tried to ignore it at first, but when the touch turned into an insistent tapping, he finally opened his eyes, ready to give the maid an earful. Instead, he was dazzled by the beautiful woman who stood by his bedside. He blinked his eyes, shut them, then opened them again to see if the apparition had disappeared. But she was right there, smiling down at him.

Petite, fair and doe-eyed, she was dressed in a red silk sari edged with gold *zari*[31] work. She wore several bangles on her wrists and carried a lotus in one hand, while using her free hand to tap him awake. Her entire body shimmered as though she'd swallowed several lightbulbs on her way to see him. Her long black tresses lay loose on her back, and she had a gold crown placed at a jaunty angle on her head.

"Who are you? How did you get in here?" Lala Lakshmi sat up, suddenly wide awake.

"Don't you recognise me?" Her voice was soft and melodious.

She looked familiar, but he couldn't place her straight away. He wondered if someone was playing a prank on him. If they were, they'd regret it. But his immediate problem was getting rid of this woman who looked like she'd escaped from a travelling drama company.

"Are you an actress?"

She smiled. "I have been known to take on several roles."

"Listen, madam... errr... *behenji*[32], I'm not sure who has put you up to this, but it's really not a good idea to walk into strange men's bedrooms at night. Whatever they are paying you, I'll pay you double. Just quit bothering me and leave now."

"What would I do with money?" She looked at him mournfully. "No one has paid me ever. I'm the one that distributes the wealth."

"So, you're an employer of some sort? Ahhh, I get it! Are you working with Hari? Is this his way of exacting revenge?"

She looked confused. "Hari? Who, my Lord? No, he has nothing to do with this. I chose this assignment for myself."

"Look, Madam, I'm tiring of your riddles. Either you leave now or I'll call the police."

She took a few steps back, looking perplexed.

"I don't understand, Lakshmi. Didn't Popat Chand give you my message?"

"Popat... My grandfather? What kind of trickery is this? How did you do all this?"

Suddenly furious, he jumped out of bed. He was being made a fool of, and he wasn't going to take it anymore. He grabbed her arm, ready to march her to the police station himself if he had to.

A 1000 volts of electricity jolted through his arm, flinging him back upon the bed. He lay on his back, panting; ears ringing, heart pounding, sweat pooling under his armpits. What had just happened?!

"Lakshmi *beta*, for someone who prays to me daily, you are not very respectful in person," she observed sadly.

He propped himself up on his arms and looked at her carefully. Could it be? But that was impossible! Or was it? On a night like this, anything was possible.

Shakily he stood up, then knelt in front of the *Devi*, head raised, eyes beseeching.

"Lakshmi *Maa*, is it really you?"

"Get up, child. Indeed, it is I."

"Blessed am I to be in your presence..." Lala Lakshmi started chanting in Sanskrit -

> *"shreerasthu*
> *hari aum*
> *naamnaam saashsahasrancha bruuhi gaargya*
>   *mahaamathe*
> *mahaalakshmyaa mahaadevyaa bhukti*
>   *mukthyardasiddhaye..."*

"Stop, child, stop. We have plenty to see and do tonight. You can do all your praying tomorrow."

His chin wobbled as he gawped at her in confusion. See? Do? What, exactly?

"You'll see, Lakshmi," she said, as though reading his mind. "Now, hop on."

Lakshmi goggled at the great white unblinking owl that had suddenly appeared out of nowhere.

"Err, *Maa*, I don't think I'll fit on there…"

"Of course you will, child. You have ridden on that tiny vehicle tonight. My owl can accommodate far more than that."

She placed herself delicately on the bird's back, inviting him to take his place behind her. Cautiously he sat down, gripping onto its large feathers, too afraid to say no, but equally afraid of what was to follow.

Closing his eyes, he prayed to *Maa* Lakshmi before he realised she was sitting right in front of him. So he clenched his eyes and his mouth and hoped that he wouldn't be tomorrow's grisly headline.

The owl took off and Lala Lakshmi did not topple off his back. A few minutes later he opened one eye and then the other. They were soaring above all the houses in his neighbourhood, rising higher and higher till the buildings were just tiny little specks on the ground.

"Where are we headed, *Maa*?"

"Nearly there, Lakshmi, just be patient for a little longer."

Slowly the great owl descended onto a quiet street in a modest neighbourhood filled with clusters of small homes. *Maa* Lakshmi walked towards one house in particular. Lala Lakshmi hurried along behind her.

The lights were on in the living room, and as they peered in through the window, he saw a plump woman dressed in a sari placing various dishes of food upon the table. She called out to someone to say that dinner was ready. Gradually the family members trooped in to take their places at the table. *Maa* Lakshmi put a finger to her lips at Lala Lakshmi's sudden intake of breath.

His grandfather sat at the head of the table, his father on his right, and a much younger Lakshmi Chand on his left. His mother, the lady in the sari, deftly placed a *chapati*[33] each on their plates, ladling out the curries and vegetables too. Her head remained covered as a mark of respect for her father-in-law. Then she retreated to the kitchen, leaving the menfolk to eat together.

The young Lakshmi Chand started to say something, but a glance from his father quelled him. They ate in silence, until unable to hold it in any more, he cried out, "I want to do Business Studies *dadaji*. It's only a two-year course in America, and they have offered me a scholarship to go."

Lala Popat Chand placed his chapati on his plate carefully, stood up and whacked Lakshmi straight across his face.

"*Bauji*[34]," his father Gopi Chand entreated, "he's just a young boy; he does not understand. I will explain it all to him..."

"Tell this no-good son of yours that he will stay in this country and work for our family business. Go to America! Pah! I tell you Gopi, if you let this boy go, you'll never get him back."

The same sense of humiliation coursed through Lala Lakshmi once again as he revisited this scene from his past. A past he had wilfully and deliberately buried in his subconscious.

Suddenly the entire neighbourhood dissolved before his eyes, and he was in a beautiful park on a spring afternoon. Lovers strolled arm-in-arm as children played cricket on the grass and families picnicked together. From a distance, he spied a young Lakshmi sitting with a girl on a bench.

Forgetting himself, he moved closer to eavesdrop on their conversation.

"Laksh, I thought we had an agreement. I've already accepted my place at Boston University. Now you're telling me you can't make it?"

"I'm sorry, Namita, but my family is adamant that I complete my education here, then join the business. It's only a matter of a few years. Then we can be together again, *na*?"

"Don't fool yourself, Laksh. If they won't even give you the freedom to study abroad, what makes you think they'll accept me as a prospective bride for you?"

"We love each other Nam, we'll find a way."

He felt a light tap on his shoulder as *Maa* Lakshmi indicated that he needed to climb onto the owl again. They flew through the sky once more, but this time Lala Lakshmi remained preoccupied by his thoughts; his fear banished by the many what-if's that jostled for space in his mind.

How would life have turned out if he'd stood up to his father and grandfather? Would he have married Namita and lived the life he'd wanted? Would he have been happy? Or, at the very least, happier than he was now?

Before he knew it, they had alighted once more. This time they were on a narrow street, with tiny houses crowding together. Without being told, Lala Lakshmi proceeded to the only house with a light shining within.

A sick child lay on a mattress on the floor, her mother wringing out and replacing the wet cloth on her forehead. Worried, she looked up at her husband.

"The fever just isn't breaking Raju. I've tried everything. I even rubbed *neem* [35]leaves on the soles of her feet. What if we lose her?" Her voice caught on a sob.

"Don't say that, Sarita. She'll be fine. I will take her to the doctor first thing tomorrow morning."

"You should have taken her today!" She blazed at him. "Instead, you ran around your Lala*ji*, even dropping him home. Raju, I cannot bear to lose another child. If anything happens to Madhu, I will die too."

"Shhhh, don't talk like that. Madhu is our little warrior. She has always been. Remember when they had given up hope when she was two months old and had contracted malaria. Didn't she recover from that? We'll get through this Sarita, I promise you we will. Now, you rest. I'll take care of her."

"But you have to go to work tomorrow."

"It's okay. Lala*ji* will understand if I'm late."

"And if he fires you?"

"Don't worry about all that. Just get some sleep now."

Lala Lakshmi watched Raju bent double with fatigue tending to the pale child who was breathing shallowly in the small one-bedroom flat. He felt ashamed of his earlier callousness. How heartless he'd been telling him to give her Crocin, dismissing a father's concern and holding him back when he should have let him go.

"Will she live?" He whispered to *Maa* Lakshmi, who just smiled enigmatically and pointed in a different direction.

He followed her to another door and another place.

This was his sister Mala's house. He saw her squatting in front of her main door, designing a beautiful *rangoli* pattern with the coloured powders she had on a plate. Garlands of marigolds hung from the doorway, and a curtain of lights covered the walls and the balconies. Children played hide and seek, squealing with excitement when someone was caught. Two old ladies sat on a *charpoy* [36]in the courtyard shelling peas and gossiping.

Just then, Madan, his brother-in-law, walked towards his wife, briefcase in one hand and a box of *mithai* in the other.

"More *mithai*? As if we don't have enough in the house already!" Mala scolded him, catching sight of the box in his hand.

"But these are only for you, my *jaan*[37]. I know how much you love *gulab jamun*[38], and you won't have to share these with anyone."

Pleased, Mala giggled and gave him a quick hug, pulling back before they were spotted displaying their affection in public.

"Any news from *bhaiyya*[39]?" She asked hopefully.

"He's not coming. Says he's too busy with the store and all the orders that are coming in. Lakshmi Chand is such a workaholic. Just once he can forget about everything and come visit his baby sister, *na*?"

Mala's face fell listening to Madan.

"*Chalo*, never mind. Maybe he'll come next year."

Lala Lakshmi felt a sudden pang of guilt. When was the last time he'd visited his sister? Not in the last five years, as far as he could recall. How could he have forgotten all about her, the only family he had left?

But *Maa* Lakshmi was already chivvying him along. This time she settled behind him on the owl. Now they were soaring over factories and godowns, areas thick with the smoke of production, the lanes narrow and potholed, the rooms confined and airless. He spied his factory in the distance. This time the owl did not land; instead it swooped low enough for him to see his workmen sweating in the heat of the single room that they worked in.

Large metal *kadhais* [40]with bubbling oil sent up acrid fumes through the air. Thin, scrawny arms sweated as they slogged in a chamber with little ventilation, under the harsh light of naked light-bulbs. He watched the men laugh, swear and curse Lala Lakshmi Chand, the *mota karela*[41], as the heat and grime rose and settled on their hair, their faces, inside their nostrils; years of servitude deposited within their hearts. When had all kindness taken leave of him, he wondered, horrified at the inhumane conditions his workers toiled in.

He turned his head to ask *Maa* Lakshmi a question, but they were already rising through the air again, and his words were whipped away by the wind.

When the owl landed in front of a grim looking building, the facade of which Lala Lakshmi knew well, he stayed seated. *Maa* Lakshmi held out her hand to him encouragingly. He placed his hand in her lotus-soft palm and allowed himself to be led into the crematorium.

He lay there on the wooden pyre, still dressed in his white *kurta* pyjama, but even fatter than he was now. The man on the pyre was morbidly obese.

Three people stood by watching as a crematorium worker lit a torch to set the pyre ablaze. The men spoke to each other in hushed whispers.

"Poor fellow died of a cardiac arrest. The maid didn't even find him till the next morning..."

"What will happen to the store now?"

"They will sell it, of course. All that money, and nobody left to even mourn him. He worked night and day for what? This?"

"*Arey baba*, I heard that the workers actually celebrated when they heard he'd died."

"Really? What a sad life. Never married, did nothing but sit in that shop day in and day out."

He watched his body go up in flames and turned his head away, unable to look or listen any further.

"Enough *Maa*! Enough. Please take me home now."

Back in his room, Lala Lakshmi touched *Devi Maa* Lakshmi's feet with a deep reverence.

"Why did you choose me *Maa*?"

"Lakshmi Chand, there are many like you that believe that I am only the goddess of wealth. That if you clean your houses and light them up, if you pray to me annually on Diwali, I will sweep into your lives with bounties of prosperity and good fortune. But, Lala Lakshmi, true wealth lies within, within the humanity everyone possesses. A life that is virtuous and balanced, is one in which all four goals of humanity are fulfilled. *Dharma* is the pursuit of an ethical and moral life, *Artha* is the pursuit of material wealth, *Kama* is the pursuit of love, and *Moksha* is the pursuit of spiritual salvation.

Together they come together as *Purusartha*, a noble life. Tell me, Lakshmi, do you feel you have led a life such as this?"

Lala Lakshmi shook his head dolefully. At some level he had always sensed that his life was incomplete, but tonight his journey had shown him just how much, and in how many ways.

"Can I still atone for my sins, *Maa*?"

"Your sins have been those of ignorance, cowardice and greed. But within you I see the capacity for great good and even greater love. My child, for twenty years I've watched you slowly strangulating the very things that give meaning and purpose to life. No, it isn't too late to atone. Do more than just atone, Lala Lakshmi. Make me proud."

With that pronouncement, *Maa* Lakshmi, the *Devi* of prosperity and enlightenment, disappeared altogether.

Lala Lakshmi sat on his bed contemplating her words. A plan started formulating in his mind. In a frenzy, he pulled off his night-shirt and took himself off to bathe.

Shaved, showered and dressed, Lala Lakshmi was ready to start his day. Then he glanced at the clock and groaned. It was only 4:15 a.m.

When Raju came in at 11 a.m. after having had Madhu checked by the doctor, and having bought the required medication from the chemists, he had his resignation letter ready in his shirt pocket. Yesterday had taught him a valuable lesson. His family was far more important than Lala*ji*'s whims, fancies and Draconian management.

He walked towards the store, puzzled to find the glass doors locked and customers lining up outside waiting to be let in. All the employees were gathered together listening to Lala*ji* talk. Someone spotted him and opened the door, ushering him inside. He walked in warily, fully expecting to be fired on the spot. Instead, Lala Lakshmi stood in front of the bronze statue of Lakshmi *Devi* with his arms outstretched.

"There he is! Raju, come in, come in. Now, stand here. Everybody, I have an announcement to make. From tomorrow Raju will be the manager of this store."

A ripple of hushed comments ran through the store employees, laced with surprise and suspicion.

"Yes, you heard right. Raju has been my right-hand man for fifteen years. This promotion is my way to repay his loyalty. From now on, you will answer to him, not me."

"But Lala*ji*," someone called out, "What are you going to do?"

"Me?" Lala Lakshmi smiled broadly. "First, I will visit my sister in Lucknow and spend Diwali with my family." He looked around the store with gleaming eyes. "Then I will go to America for a holiday."

Everyone gasped. Lala Lakshmi and holiday?

"When I come back next year..."

"Next year?!"

"Yes, next year, I am going to open a new factory that will be just as modern as this store here. Then I will open a school and a medical centre for all my employees. After that, who knows? With *Maa* Lakshmi's blessings, I may be able to do so much more."

Raju stood still next to his *sahib*, wondering when someone would yell that it was all a joke and that he really had been fired.

Lala Lakshmi turned around to him and spoke gently, "I know it's a lot to take in Raju, but I have full faith in you. You'll be able to do it. Now, take today off and go home. Go celebrate with your family. And here, give this to your little girl."

Lala Lakshmi gave him a thin gold chain with a small pendant of the goddess Lakshmi on it.

Tears ran down Raju's face as he kneeled to touch Lala*ji*'s feet. Unable to articulate his gratitude, he simply kept moving his hands from Lala*ji*'s feet to his own forehead.

"Stop that, Raju. I should be the one thanking you for your long and loyal service. If it weren't for you, this store wouldn't be what it is. Now, please open the doors before those crowds break them down."

Raju quietly made his way to the glass doors, opening them as Lala*ji* had instructed. Hordes of customers swarmed in, eager to buy the famous *mithai* from Popat Chand Mithaiwala. As Raju slipped out from the side, he turned to see Lala Lakshmi mouth something at him.

Later, back in his home, after he had told his shocked wife everything and given his daughter the gold necklace, he realised what Lala*ji* had been saying.

Smiling to himself, he responded quietly in his mind.

"Happy Diwali."

An homage to Charles Dickens' 'A Christmas Carol'

8

—————

A THANK YOU WOULD BE NICE

If you were to look at me, you would never be able to tell how angry I am. Not just angry, but raging! Infuriated with everything - with the ungrateful people that occupy this planet, infuriated with myself for taking my youth for granted, and most of all, infuriated that I no longer understand where I fit in this rapidly changing world.

But, if you were to look at me, assuming you spared me a passing glance, you would see an attractive, slightly thickset middle-aged woman, who has resorted to wearing ugly yet comfortable shoes but still likes to dress fashionably. You might even glance a second time at my face, which had once been a part of several promotional photographs for the airline I still work for. That is, until younger and more attractive faces replaced me.

I try. I truly do try. I get regular facials; I use a gadget that sends micro currents into the dermis to stimulate collagen. I've even succumbed to the occasional Botox treatment. However, the march of time carries on upon my face and body, and who am I kidding? Everyone can see that I am no spring chicken.

At the gym, where I once stood front and centre in the punishing classes euphemistically named "Recharge, Renew or Attack", I now lurk at the back, panting my way through the forty-five minute sessions. I watch as young and nubile bodies preen in the mirrors while they lift twice the amount of weight I am capable of, with the ease that I once had. I feel like smacking their perky bottoms.

Sixty-two years old, and I have achieved the impossible. I am alive —breathing, walking, talking—and I am invisible. Invisible to the point that if I walked out of my front door naked, no one would bat an eyelid.

Gosh, that makes me angry! So bloody angry.

This rage is like a living thing; palpitating beneath my skin's surface, coursing through my veins, pounding in my head and clenching its hands around my heart, squeezing it so hard that some days I want to cry out from the pain of it.

What's the point? Who would hear me if I cried?

Loneliness, my constant companion, is a quiet friend. She hides in the nooks and crannies of my life, emerging in unexpected moments. That beautiful evening which I yearn to share with a husband, that spa day that I'd want my daughter to be with me for, or even that solitary lunch when I look over and see a group of girl-friends giggling over glasses of wine.

Perhaps it's in my nature that I could never hold on to a relationship. I've flitted in and out of amorphous affairs, much after the solid kinships, the ones I thought were mine for life, left me adrift.

Then there is my job, which has always taken me away from home for long stretches of time. And while I have been somewhere up in the air, people's lives have carried on without me. My colleagues, themselves creatures of uncertain rosters and victims of jet lag, have been just as fragmentary and capricious in their concomitance. Companions for an evening and then off again to another flight, another shore, another schedule.

When people say that flying is a young person's job, I turn around and say that life itself is a young person's domain. As children, we are subject to our guardians' rules and protocols, and as the elderly, we are relegated to anonymity, shoved aside by a world that prizes youth above all else.

Doesn't that make you mad?

At fifty, when my internal thermostat set itself to Saharan temperatures, a furnace igniting inside of me, a young gay man said to me in jest that I was a "menopausal bitch". He said it was in jest, but there was a malicious glee that underpinned those words, and boy, did they hit home!

What had I done to be accused so grievously? I had upbraided him for doing shoddy work on the plane. He had gotten back at me in the way men have behaved towards women for eons, by attacking my age, my gender and a time in my life which I had little control over. A time when I could have done with some understanding and tenderness, instead of the casual disdain of a man who was more of a bitch than I could ever be.

Ten years later, I am no closer to forgiving him.

Men. What a waste of time they have been! From my father, who only ever belittled the women in his life, to the many boyfriends who wanted a beautiful young woman in their arms, but only if she was vacant between the ears—I learned pretty early on that the best way to get on in a world that is skewed heavily in favour of men, is to pretend.

Pretend to be silly, to be obedient and subservient, to listen and obey, to never overstep the mark, to treat each man as if the sun shone out of his backside. Believe you me, every man thinks it does! And while that breathless bimbo act served me satisfactorily for years, something else was itching to get out. Something that stayed hidden well into my fifties, and then, when it did burst out, it nearly destroyed me.

In my sixties, I nurture that rage, keeping it under wraps, but tending to it like a favourite pet. It keeps me alive, it gives me purpose, and while the acid of it eats at me internally, it is the very fuel that propels me forward too.

Yes, I am an ageing, overweight flight attendant. I am one of the several you might see dragging a case behind her as she dodders her way to the airport gate in her orthopaedic shoes, the one you might casually shove aside in the Starbucks queue because you are in a hurry and your time is more important than hers, the one you ignore and dismiss on the aircraft, your eyes drawn to the pretty young thing in the next aisle. Yes, I am one of those utterly forgettable women of a certain age, the ones that society cannot wait to be rid of, the ones that younger colleagues constantly exhort: "Retire, why don't you, senior mama? You've done your time. Let us enjoy this career now!"

I am a 'senior mama' flight attendant. I am also a serial killer.

"What have you done with your hair, Elaine?" Lisa smiles that fake smile of hers while pouring coffee into her styrofoam cup. She is doing the First Class galley today, and I know it's going to be a long night.

"Brushed it?" I wink, hoping humour will cover my irritation.

"Oh, you're so funny!" She giggles, adding half-and-half to the coffee, then reaching for the sugar. I nearly stop her, but hold back. It's none of my business if she wants to go up to size twenty-two in her uniform. The dress she is in is bursting at the seams anyway. It's embarrassing, but hey, not my problem!

I pick up the interphone to make a PA, calling everyone to First Class for their briefing. The pilots have yet to board, but I know this Captain, and once he gets started on his briefing, I won't get a word in. Best get mine done first, and quickly.

I start by handing everyone their position sheets. If they've done their homework, they will know where they are working, where to stow their luggage and what their safety checks are. But there's always one who needs spoon feeding. Cue that thought, Julie pipes up.

"Elaine, must I do the meal orders?"

"That's what the briefing sheet says, Julie." I smile tightly, knowing exactly what's coming next.

"But you're the Purser! Why don't you do it?"

"Fine, I'll do it." I submit graciously because I really don't mind doing it. It gives me a chance to greet everyone in First Class and get a measure of them too.

"Right! Breaks next. Who wants what?"

They squabble amongst themselves for the second break, but the seniors win out as usual. Since I am the most senior, I've put myself down for second break, Bunk 3. There have to be some perks to having flown for forty-one years.

Just then, the Captain walks in with the two First Officers trailing behind.

"Ah, Elaine!" He booms, his handlebar moustache quivering. "Good to see you again. Hair's looking fancy!"

I touch my hair self-consciously, wondering what everyone else is seeing, that I'm not.

"Ready to brief, Captain?" I smile at him.

He looks around, his eyes settling on Juanita.

"We are a team. You are my eyes and ears out here..." He drones on, and I could recite the whole thing off by heart. His briefing hasn't changed in the thirty-odd years that I've known him. But today he's got a new girl to impress, and his eyes are fairly caressing her. Juanita is simpering under all the attention. Silly girl. He'll probably wine and dine her in London, bed her, and then forget all about her. Seen it all far too many times. I suppress a yawn.

"Three black coffees to the cockpit," the First Officer mutters at me as he walks past. What a charmer!

The first few minutes of boarding are always chaotic. The greeter is at the door, but I'm being pulled in all directions. The ground staff want to talk to me about the unaccompanied minors, Economy galley is still being boarded, the Captain is asking about his meals, and Lisa is moaning about half her galley items missing. All this, and I'm trying to get the meal orders sorted.

The first person I approach is an Asian lady in her fifties.

"Mrs Chen, what would you like to eat today?"

She waves me off, as if I'm an irritating mosquito. Right, she'll just have to wait then, and maybe, when I do get around to her, her meal choice might not be available. Ho Hum! That's the way the cookie crumbles.

The next few people are nice enough. Savvy flyers, they give me their meal orders quickly; smiling and polite. My favourite kind of passengers. It's all going well. Too well. Something terrible is bound to happen, and then it does.

Julie is holding a tray of orange juice and sparkling wine, trying to serve people even as passengers board and stow their luggage. Although most of us are adept at dodging people and bags while accomplishing our pre-departure tasks, accidents occur occasionally. Even as I lean over to ask the man in 4A his meal choice, another man pushes past with his rucksack, hitting Julie's tray and sending it flying, soaking the man sitting on 4C, who jumps up and lets loose a volley of invectives. Holy crap! Here we go.

"Mr Williams, I am so sorry!" I say.

Julie has already rushed back to the galley for wet towels, and I'm left holding the baby. A furious, six-foot-tall baby.

"What kind of shitty service is this? I'm attending a meeting in London tomorrow morning! Look at my jacket." He is turning purple now.

I try calming him.

"Mr Williams, I will issue you with dry cleaning vouchers, and give you two thousand miles credit towards your next trip as well. Julie will clean your jacket as best as she can. I'm terribly sorry about this accident. We will do our best to ensure that the rest of your flight goes well." I am grovelling now, and Julie is trying to pat him down ineffectually with the towels.

He bats her hands off and turns to me.

"I will be complaining to your CEO about this. I am a Platinum member, and I'll make sure neither of you has a job by the end of the day."

I sigh internally. Yes, I've heard this several times over the course of my career. What Mr Williams, Platinum member of the Asshole Club doesn't know is that as a unionised member, even the CEO can't remove me from my job unless I commit murder on the plane.

Which I very well might...

I always give people enough rope to hang themselves. That is to say, enough opportunities to redeem themselves before my internal barometer decides that enough is enough. So, I allow Mr Williams to let off steam as I ply him with champagne and try to soothe his frayed nerves.

Flight attendants, for the most part, are amongst the most empathetic people you will find in any profession. Just look at us. We are nurses and nannies, lifesavers and counsellors. We are trained to fight fires, give CPR and evacuate a plane in 90 seconds. We are also privy to inflight proposals and engagements, fights and break-ups, and the many fools who want to join the Mile High Club with their sexcapades. And, if you've flown as long as I have, you've pretty much seen it all. I know I have. Let me tell you, the human species does not impress me much. We are a sorry bunch.

What gets me the most is how dismissive people are about our profession. Remember the last crash that happened? That crew was amazing! They evacuated a planeload of people in under a minute with barely any casualties. Guess who got all the kudos? The pilots, of course! The 'trolley dollies' weren't even worth a mention.

Trolley dolly, cart tart, galley hag, sky muffin, air mattress, latrine queen - aren't they just full of praise for us? Yet another thing that makes my blood boil!

So, here's Mr Williams, full of self-importance, embodying the two qualities that I cannot stand in a man - misogyny and disrespect. Patronising me every step of the way, he's treating me like a used slipper. And what do I do? I smile and submit to the mistreatment, reminding myself that he still has a few chances left.

·　·　·

When I say I'm a serial killer, I'm no Ted Bundy. I choose my victims carefully, after much deliberation. I'm canny enough to know that I can't commit a murder on every flight. That would be insane, and suicidal. So, I space them out over months with no discernible pattern. The modus operandi remains the same. If the passenger has been a giant pain in the rear, and I see no redeeming qualities in him whatsoever, then I slip a bit of my 'magic potion' into his meal. Odourless, tasteless and slow-acting, it often takes a week for it to fell the victim. The symptoms are so varied that even the doctors are unable to diagnose the person before it's too late. By which time, he's dead and I am one satisfied bunny.

Now, you may well ask, how do I know if the deed is done? Don't forget, as the Purser, I have all the details of his itinerary, his address and his status with my airline. I'm smart enough to track him discreetly and see him meet his sticky end. And come on, with social media, nothing is private anymore, is it? Even death has an audience.

As for the 'magic potion', suffice to say it was a discovery I made in Brazil many years ago. At the time, I was looking for a way to end things for myself. Then I decided it would be far more fun and cathartic to rid the earth of the human vermin that inhabit it.

In the last decade, I've probably killed around fifteen people, give or take. Most of them men. There's been a few women too, but I always give more latitude to my own sex. I know how hard it is as a woman to survive in this world, and unless she is a colossal bitch with no chance at redemption, I normally let her off. The two I didn't, just caught me on a bad day, I guess. Sorry, not sorry.

Mr Williams now has the glazed look of a man who has mixed his drinks with impunity. He started with the champagne, switched to a red wine with his steak, drank a glass and a half of port with his cheese, and is rounding off the proceedings with a double gin and tonic. Maybe he'll just end up alcohol poisoning himself, sparing me a whole lot of trouble.

You see, he's skating on very thin ice right now. He's become louder and more obnoxious with every course. He's spilt his wine all over himself, and now looks like a patchwork quilt of alcohol. No doubt, he'll blame that on us, too. Julie has flat out refused to serve him, leaving me to manage Mr Platinum Idiot.

"Mr Williams," I shake him, not sure whether to clear his half-eaten dessert. He seems asleep, his mouth open, a bit of mashed gateau still visible in it. I shake him again, and he wakes with a start.

"Wh... wha...?"

"Are you done with your dessert, sir?"

Something about the sight of me enrages him. He lunges at me, forgetting he's still got his seat belt on. I jump back in alarm. But there's a look in his eyes that tells me that this is not a happy drunk. I rush back to the galley, pick up the phone to call the cockpit and warn them about a disruptive passenger. I can still see him struggling with his belt, and I yell to Lisa, "Get the handcuffs, 4C is losing it!"

The passengers are all turning to look at him. I grab the nearest thing I can find to defend myself, an ice mallet, and hold it up. I don't rate my chances against a six-foot hulk, but adrenalin is surging through me, and I intend to bash him with everything I've got.

The next few moments seem to pass as if in a dream. Even as the Captain answers the phone and I garble out the situation, Mr Williams gets up from his seat, his eyes focussed on me. Then slowly, and with great deliberateness, he lowers his trousers and his underwear, squats in the middle of the aisle and defecates, not once removing his eyes from my face.

The interphone drops out of my hand as I watch him, stunned.

Wow.

We all look at him, speechless with disgust. Of course, we will divert. He will be arrested. He might even get a bit of prison time if not an enormous fine. But none of that is punishment enough.

What he doesn't know is that now he's pissed me off royally! Enough to make him my sixteenth victim. I look at him squatting in the aisle, and shake my head ever so slightly.

You just blew your last chance right there, buddy.

I wasn't always an embittered, angry woman. I started out like any other young girl with stars in her eyes, vowing to myself that I'd allow no man to treat me in the manner that my father had treated my mother. It was quite obvious in our household that a woman's place was in the kitchen, with an apron over her pretty dress, her hair always perfectly coiffed and Revlon's 'Cherries in the Snow' applied on her lips and nails. I wanted to escape that fate.

When I applied and got accepted as a trainee flight attendant, my father disowned me, not wanting to have anything to do with a woman training to be a tart. Or some such thing. In his eyes, flight attendants were no better than prostitutes, with loose morals and looser panties. My mother, as always, hid behind his opinions, too scared to support me the one time I really needed her to.

So, I packed my bags and left.

Several years later, when I returned to meet her after my father's death, the mousy woman I'd left behind had transformed into a fake-tanned, plump and cheerful woman, remarried to a used-car salesman who obviously adored her. The transformation was so startling that I stuttered my way through a stilted conversation and never went back to see her again. Nor did she ask me to. Our lives by then had bifurcated in separate directions, anyway.

My early days of flying were filled with exotic destinations, lots of champagne, and men who couldn't wait to take me out. There was plenty of hard work but also plenty of glamour. We were the next best thing to film stars, and as we walked through airports en masse in our tight little skirts, hats jauntily perched on our heads, every eye would turn to watch us.

However, things were changing in our industry at the time and the old-timers, used to carrying ball gowns in their suitcases and being wined and dined at embassies the world over, warned us with doom-laden voices that it was all going downhill rapidly. Their complaints: longer working hours, shorter layovers, the wrong kind of people finding their way onto aircraft. None of us newbies heeded their warnings. Why would we? We were having a whale of a time, and the way we looked at it, these ancient women (who were only in their thirties but seemed decades older) were just trying to rain on our youthful parade.

Every generation that sees the world change around them tries to warn the next one. But to the generation that is living it, this is their reality and all those warnings are just like shouting into the wind. So it went with us. The old-timers either got married and left, or carried on flying with us, complaining bitterly about every new development or innovation.

Yes, times were changing, but for the better. Those old, archaic rules of having to leave after marriage or having babies were soon scrapped. In time, we would see the age and weight limits disappear too. So really, if anything, I chose the best time to join the best industry.

But if this were a fairytale, I'd be skipping into the sunset with my handsome prince rather than slipping a little something into a cup of tea for a handcuffed, six-foot-tall, barely-in-his-senses passenger who stank to high heaven.

Flying was a dream job for me, and I gave it my all for most of my twenties. When I met Craig on a red-eye, I didn't expect that he would be "The One". But unlike other men who had their fun and moved on to more domesticated women, Craig loved my independence and the fact that I was financially solvent. "Marry me, fly free!" I used to tease him until one day he slipped a ring on my finger and shut me up for good.

There are two kinds of men that marry flight attendants. The first are the deluded sort. They have no idea what they've signed up for: the long absences, the wife who returns home tired and grumpy, the middle-of-the-night phone calls pulling her out to fly to Idaho, the absences on birthdays, anniversaries and Christmases, the lack of home-cooked meals and the sheer loneliness of being married to an absentee spouse.

Fortunately, Craig was the second kind. His aunt had flown for Pan Am and he knew exactly what he was signing up for. For five years, we had the best time together. Many a time, he would hop on a plane with me to fly to some silly destination so that we could have another mini-honeymoon. He didn't care if we were in a pokey motel or a five-star hotel as long as we were together.

So many of my colleagues would tell me I had lucked out in finding such a great guy. I truly believed I had, too. Here was a man who encouraged me to keep flying, a man who expected nothing but a bit of love and attention when I was home; a man who was willing to cook and clean in my absence, with not one word of reproach if I missed an important date in the calendar because of my schedule.

Yes, Craig was wonderful, and my memories of those days still retain a rosy glow about them. But you know what they say - when things seem too good to be true, they are. Clichés are clichés for a reason; they contain a kernel of truth within them.

Sweating, panting, and in agony as I pushed my infant out of my vagina, Craig picked that exact moment to tell me he'd been having an affair and was going to leave me.

Bastard! Wish I'd poisoned him, too.

Our layover in London has been cut short by Platinum Asshole's shitty shenanigans.

I'm not bothered. I've been to London a gazillion times and don't care for it. It rains all the time, and the people are polite but miserable-looking. Everything is grey - from the buildings to the weather to the monarchy. At least in the Diana days, I could spend my time with a Hello magazine that followed her every move. Now, I don't even bother putting the television on. My iPad and Netflix get me through the most boring of layovers.

Still, an invitation to the bar is a welcome distraction. Captain

Handlebar has called us all for a liquid debriefing. He figures we need it after the horrendous time we had on the flight. I will not pass up an opportunity to watch a pilot actually put his hand in his pocket for the crew. Most of them are such miserly bastards they even take the soft drinks off the plane.

"Tim was asking about you," he says to me while handing me a glass of white wine.

"Really?" I just lift an eyebrow.

"He still thinks about you, you know Elaine."

"How's his wife?"

That shuts him up for a bit. He knocks back his beer and heads back to the bar for another one.

I look around. Almost everyone is down here, except for Lisa, who is a snap, click, shut-the-door kind of gal. We never see her on layovers, and I know that a lot of us old-timers are categorised as boring by the young ones. What they don't know is the amount of partying we did back in the day. Lisa was one of the wildest ones, rumoured to have dated a sheikh who gifted her with a Rolex watch. I can believe it. She was a stunner in her day, but time and age have taken a toll on her body, and these days all she does is complain about her ungrateful children and eat her way across the Atlantic.

Julie plonks herself next to me.

"I'm so tired Elaine!"

"Didn't you nap?"

"I couldn't sleep. I just kept thinking of that awful man. What a disgusting thing to do!"

"He claimed he had no memory of it."

"What?!"

"Said he took an Ambien before dinner."

"And then mixed it with alcohol? Do you believe him?"

I shrug.

"They'll let him off with a slap on the wrist."

What he doesn't know is that within a week, he'll wish he was in prison, because that would be a better fate than what awaits him.

"How can you be so calm? I'm still fuming at the way he behaved!"

That's rich, particularly as she left me to handle him. But Julie and I go back a long way, so I smile at her and say, "You have to roll with the punches in this job, don't you?"

"Ma was asking about you the other day. Ever since you've moved, we've hardly seen you. Why don't you come around one of these days?"

I take a gulp of my wine, trying to hide my guilt. It's true that I've sort of abandoned Mrs Allen and Julie in the last two years. How can I explain that visiting them is like revisiting a painful past?

Just then, Captain Handlebar returns with his beer and sits down with us. I wonder why he's ignoring Juanita, then notice that she's getting plenty of attention from the two First Officers. Guess he realises when he's outnumbered. But they'll pay for it tomorrow, they just don't know it yet.

"I was just saying, Chuck, that that awful man needs to go to prison for a long, long time! Those poor cleaners. What a job they have ahead of them." Julie makes a sad face, then leans forward and taps his wrist. "You were so smart to divert to Logan."

"We were lucky! Over the Atlantic it would have been far more difficult."

"Lucky they had a replacement plane too," I say, noting Julie crossing and uncrossing her legs. When will she learn?

Captain Handlebar turns to me.

"I just had a message from Tim. He said to say 'hi' to you."

"Okay."

"Don't you want to say anything in return?"

"No," I lean back in my seat, "not really."

"You women can be so cold-hearted."

At Julie's sharp intake of breath, I set my drink down carefully on the coaster in front of me.

"Chuck, I wasn't the one stringing someone along for nearly ten years, complaining about how miserable I was and how I was going to leave my wife as soon as... wait..." I tick off the reasons on my fingers, "I've paid off the house, the kids are a little older, my son's graduated, my daughter is married..."

I pick up my drink.

"So, no, I have no more time to waste on Tim. If that offends him or you, then that's just too bad."

Captain Handlebar lets out a long, low whistle.

"I'll let him know."

"Do."

He squirms in his seat, then decides that since the atmosphere will not thaw anytime soon, he might as well make himself scarce.

"You told him!" Julie looks at me, awestruck.

"Yeah, I did."

"Good for you. I never liked that weaselly Tim, anyway. What did you ever see in him?"

"Dunno. Comfort? Security? A father for Cathy?"

We both fall silent then.

She puts her hand on mine.

"How is she?"

What can you do when the one person you love the most in the world turns around and tells you she doesn't love you? What can you do when the job that puts food on the table and pays for the school fees is held up as the ogre that took you away from her? How can you explain to a child who insists on blaming you for everything that went wrong in her life, that you tried your best? And that your best wasn't good enough.

Looking back, Cathy's rebellion started young. Every time I was on an extended trip, I would return to reports from the school about her truancy, her being rude to the teachers or hitting another child. When I'd ask her why, she'd shrug and turn away. I never thought that one day all that angst would boomerang onto me.

Her unhappiness manifested itself in many ways - running away from school, dabbling in drugs and alcohol early on, and tattoos and piercings I vocally disapproved of. But there was a tender side to her that melted me each time. The way she would come and hug me from behind, the flowers she'd pick for me on the way back from school, the shoulder massages she'd give me after particularly hard night flights.

I still remember Julie's mother, Mrs Allen, who had babysat Cathy from a young age, saying to me, "It's not you she hates, it's your job. You are the only constant in her life, and every time you go away, she doesn't know when or even if you'll return. That can mess with a child's mind."

What was I to do? Give up the only job I was qualified for and live on food stamps, or carry on flying and give my daughter the childhood she deserved? I tried showing her in every way possible that I loved her. Through phone calls that cost me the earth, through trips to Paris and Rome, through trying to be there for the important milestones in her life. Yet once her teenage brain had decided that I was the culprit, nothing was going to change her mind.

Then there was Tim, the substitute father for ten years, who dipped in and out of our lives as he pleased. When I eventually finished with him after reaching the grim realisation that I would always be the mistress and never the wife, Cathy blamed me for that, too.

"How is she?" I ponder the question, staring into the bottom of my wine glass. "I wish I knew, Julie. She doesn't keep in touch."

"Even after all these years?"

I nod sadly.

"But you do know where she is, right? I mean, what if something happens? How would the company contact her? She's your next of kin."

"She doesn't want me in her life. What can I do about that?"

"You know," Julie swirls the lemon in her drink contemplatively, "she sent us a Christmas card last year, completely out of the blue."

I lean forward, interested now. It's been years since she's been in contact with anyone from the past.

"I think she has a little boy. It was signed 'Cathy and Noah'. Unless that's her new boyfriend." She looks at me, questions in her eyes.

"No, the boyfriend's name was Matt. Noah is her son. He must be around four now."

"How do you know all this?"

"I follow her Instagram page."

"Doesn't it just kill you to know that you have a grandson?"

"In more ways than you can imagine, Julie," I sigh, tearfully.

It had been a Milan Three-Day, and my phone got stolen somewhere near the Duomo. It's always bothered me whether the fact that I couldn't ring her on that trip precipitated her actions. When I returned home, she had vanished. There was nothing—no forewarning, no note—nothing to say where she'd gone or with whom. Contacting the cops proved useless. She was twenty-one, an adult capable of making her own decisions. That she had taken half her wardrobe with her along with her favourite Bob Dylan poster, showed that it was a premeditated act.

How long had she been planning to leave? Had life really been that insufferable under my roof? Was I really that awful a mother? These questions have plagued me for the last twelve years.

Someone once told me we don't make the mistakes our parents made, but we sure as heck make new ones. I never claimed to be perfect, but I loved Cathy with every cell in my body, and somehow, that still wasn't enough.

One of the First Officers comes and sits next to us. Frank. The one who had asked for the black coffees; the one who barely spoke to us during the flight. Clearly Juanita has picked a winner for the evening and Frank isn't it.

"Hey," he nods, looking morose.

"Welcome to the pity party," I chuckle, blinking back my tears.

That's when he looks up and sees me for the first time.

He's handsome in a sort of young Tom Cruise manner. The other guy must be a real smooth talker if Juanita picked him over this one.

"What a day and a half!" Frank says, suddenly realising that our day has been going on for a lot longer than 24 hours. That's what time difference does to your body clock.

"Yeah, it's definitely been one of those days." Julie says.

"You ladies must have seen your fair share of stuff?" he asks, genuinely curious now that he's established that we aren't multi-headed Hydras, just flight attendants who are a little riper than the average nymphet.

"I could write a book!" Julie responds.

"I wouldn't bother," I say. "No one cares about what we have to say."

"Oh come on, Elaine, even you have to admit we have the juiciest stories. Remember the time that action hero took that woman to the lavatory in First Class? Then he pretended not to know her for the rest of the flight! Her face!!"

Soon they are both trading stories, and I lean back and close my eyes. I wonder how Mr Platinum Shit is getting on.

Anger is just hurt, layered over hurt, layered over more hurt. The pain of Cathy's abandonment was far worse than anything I had ever experienced before. Searching for her proved fruitless, and in an era when anyone could be found by means of social media, she disappeared so entirely from my life it was like an amputation. Removing every trace of herself from all the places she knew I'd look, her message to me was clear enough. She didn't want me in her life.

That was when I took myself to Brazil, searching for a way to end it all. I found myself at the feet of Christ the Redeemer, and while people around me contorted their bodies in unimaginable ways to get the perfect photograph, I just stood there, mute and weeping.

Life wasn't worth living if there was no one to share it with. Realistically, I had always known that Cathy would have a life of her own one day, but it was one that I had hoped I would have some role in. To be forsaken so completely was devastating. I had fled to Brazil on a vacation that she should have been a part of. It was here that I meant to finish myself. All my affairs were in order. Cathy would inherit everything, provided they were more successful in tracing her than I had been.

The giant, imposing figure of *Cristo Redentor* glowered down at me, the sun casting long shadows from high in the sky. The day was beautiful and the excited babble of the surrounding tourists reminded me once again that this was supposed to be the trip of a lifetime, where we had planned to celebrate her 21st birthday together.

Later, as I wandered on Copacabana beach, watching people of all shapes and sizes revel in the buzzing electric energy of Rio de Janeiro, I wondered how my life had come to this. I sat watching two young girls play with a beach ball, as I let the sand run through my fingers. It was late afternoon, and I had still to locate the *kumuā*, the indigenous shaman I had stumbled upon during my research. At first, it had been for healing, but now I craved oblivion. In my pocket were 5000 Brazilian Reals, an amount that could turn even the most principled person's head, or so I hoped. There was a danger in carrying so much money in a city infested with crime but I did not care. If someone knifed me to get at it, it would all be over either way. In the cruellest of ironies, no one paid me, a middle-aged woman wandering the streets of Rio, the slightest bit of attention.

There is a song that goes - "wherever I lay my hat, that's my home..." That's true for all of us flight attendants. New environs don't make us nervous. We are so used to different countries and cultures that we fit in seamlessly wherever we go, our chameleon-like abilities undetectable to even ourselves. Hence, in Brazil, I became one of the Brazilians. With my dark hair and tendency to tan, I could fit in anywhere in the diverse ethnic and cultural spectrum of the people that inhabited this land.

I walked, unseen and unseeing, my mind a swirl of jumbled thoughts; my heart so full of pain that it felt as heavy as lead. On a scrap of paper, the hotel receptionist had drawn a crude map, after being unsuccessful in dissuading me from walking to this insalubrious part of the city. Finally, I stood before a faded green door and knocked on it forcefully.

A bent old lady opened the door, her face so lined it was impossible to tell how old she truly was. Two thin plaits trailed down her back, and she was dressed in the traditional indigenous attire of a colourful tunic and beads. She ushered me in without question, leading me through a cool hallway into the presence of the shaman, who seemed even older than her. Seated on a mat in the centre of a dark room, he barely acknowledged my presence as I walked in behind the old woman. She indicated that I should take the low stool placed before him. Then she disappeared into one of the many doors that led off the room.

I sat, nervous about articulating what had brought me to him. But before I could say anything, he spoke in heavily accented English.

"You want cure for pain?"

I nodded my head vigorously, unable to speak, unshed tears glistening in my eyes.

"Pain here?" He pointed to the centre of his chest.

"Yes," I whispered.

He peered at me in the gloom.

"You want finish?"

I nodded once again.

He stood up slowly and shuffled over to a dark corner of the room. I heard drawers opening and closing, and shut my eyes momentarily. Then I felt his presence in front of me, a faint woody smell emanating from his faded tunic. He held out his hand, and two glass vials sat in his palm.

"This heal," he pointed to the left one. "This finish," he pointed to the right one. "You choose."

I took the 5000 Reals and placed them on the mat. He barely glanced at the money, his eyes still focussed on me. I dropped my eyes under his penetrating gaze.

"One drop only," he remarked cryptically before turning away from me.

I suppose you can guess that I didn't take the one that would finish me. Instead, the one drop that healed was enough to set me on this course in life. My heart still hurt, but it was somewhat bandaged by the shaman's mysterious potion. Enough to let me live and wreak my own kind of vengeance against those who wronged or dismissed me.

Six months later, I encountered the same young man who had called me a "menopausal bitch" some years ago. On an impulse, I added a few drops of the killing potion to his coffee even as we traded banalities. Heard of overkill? That's what I did to him. He was taken off the flight on a stretcher, his body twisted; his face frozen in a terrified rictus.

That was very nearly my undoing. But when the poison proved untraceable, I decided that I would have to be much more careful in the future. And I have been very, very careful.

It's not like we don't encounter awful people daily. In my line of work, where I meet thousands of people in any given month, think of the proportion that are truly terrible. And even I know that killing all those people is a sure-fire route to prison or the mental asylum.

So, how do I gauge who is worth letting go and who needs to go? Whatever the healing potion contained, it gave me a strange sort of insight into people. There are those who are nasty because their lives contain no joy, there are those who are just having a bad day, and then there are those who have just had some event that has turned their lives upside down. I can understand them acting out, being horrible because that is their only outlet. Even if I don't condone their behaviour, I understand it. Those I can forgive. Those I let go.

It's the other ones, the ones who are arrogant enough to believe that they are better than everyone else, especially the people who serve them. The ones who treat everyone around them like garbage because they have the money, power and status to do so. It's them I can't forgive.

Ingratitude is a terrible vice. A simple thank-you can atone for so much, but it's too beneath their dignity to thank someone who they perceive as inferior.

Our jobs don't define us. They are one part of us, one part of the whole. We all deserve respect; we deserve recognition and gratitude. We deserve to be treated as equals.

"How long will this impasse continue?" Julie asks me the next day on the flight home.

"Impasse?"

"Between you and Cathy?"

"Until she decides to end it."

"What if she decides never?"

"Then so be it."

A mother's heart can contain love and hurt in equal measures. If Cathy ever reaches out to me, a dose of the healing potion awaits her. Maybe it will mend whatever fissure there is between us. But if she never does, then a small dose of the killing potion is set aside for me. Before I am caught by the law, or by disease, I will end it all.

Until then, my work of cleaning the skies of ungrateful, offensive, hideous passengers will carry on.

"You are a strange one, Elaine!" Julie looks at me, wonderingly.

"You betcha!" I laugh, and set about getting the paperwork ready for landing.

Somewhere, Mr Platinum Pants is inching towards his demise, and I have no iota of remorse or regret. Each one of us has to die, one way or another, one day or another. He just brought forward the date of his own departure thanks to his abhorrent behaviour. What did Edith Piaf sing? *Non, je ne regrette rien.* I sincerely have zero regrets.

Oh, and for the record, my name isn't really Elaine. So, the next time you fly, careful how you treat the flight attendant. A thank-you would be nice, a little bit of gratitude would go a long, long way indeed. Or, who knows what might find its way into your food and drink?

Adios, for now. I have miles to fly before I sleep.

~

THE END

Did you enjoy this book? Like to read another one like it? Give Twelve - stories from around the world a try!

AFTERWORD

Word-of-mouth is crucial for any author to succeed and if you found this book interesting *please* do leave a review on your preferred retailer. Even if it's just a star rating or a sentence or two, it would make all the difference and would be very much appreciated!!

If you enjoyed this book, you can sign up to hear more about my new releases and any special offers!

Do visit www.poornimamanco.com to keep abreast of all my news.

GLOSSARY

1. The Invisible Suitcase

1. So!
2. Used as a mild, generally humorous substitute for 'shit'.
3. A term of endearment
4. Magnificent
5. Look!
6. Coffee with milk
7. Yes
8. Darling
9. My God!
10. But no
11. Hot chocolate
12. Little cakes made with almond flour
13. Okay?
14. No
15. Their hearts
16. You are a cynic!
17. Almost certainly
18. What stupidity!
19. Small round cakes with a meringue-like consistency, made with egg white, sugar, and powdered almonds and consisting of two halves sandwiching a creamy filling.
20. A small pastry consisting of many thin layers of puff pastry, filled with custard
21. I'm sorry!
22. Very light pastry made with egg, typically used for eclairs and profiteroles.
23. Custard
24. Why not?
25. Sure!
26. Great lady
27. Yes?
28. A spread of finely chopped or pureed seasoned meat.
29. Good girl!
30. Person
31. Negatives
32. I am very talented
33. Excuse me
34. Delicious!
35. Who cares?

36. My sweet
37. I know
38. Good
39. Everything indicated that it would be done
40. Crazy!
41. Thunderbolt
42. A fiasco

2. Osterhase

1. Grandma
2. Grandpa
3. An Easter Lamb cake
4. Mother
5. Easter bunny
6. There are no eggs?
7. Hurry up!
8. Yes sir
9. Don't you have any friends?
10. Ask me!
11. Cheese with chives
12. Orange juice
13. Yummy!
14. No!
15. Darling
16. Do you need anything?
17. No, darling.

3. The Butterfly Effect

1. Grandfather
2. Butterfly (Spanish)
3. Darling
4. A ward, quarter, or district of a city or town
5. Grandmother
6. An event in which several people gather to dance tangos
7. A small, square concertina or accordion with buttons instead of a keyboard, used especially in Latin America for tango music.
8. Father
9. Princess
10. Teacher
11. Caramel sauce
12. Precious
13. Social benefits

14. The castellano word that refers to the nod of the head that is used to signal the offer and acceptance of dances at a milonga.
15. Coffee with milk
16. Breakfast pastry, a sweet croissant
17. Argentinian slang used to describe someone who is extremely annoying, an idiot or a prick.
18. Girl, or little girl.
19. an interjection commonly used to signify "hey!", "fellow", "guy".
20. Ecstatic
21. Cinema
22. Yerba mate, a traditional drink
23. In Argentine tango dancing it means "the way out (onto the dance floor)."
24. Resolution
25. The submarino (meaning "submarine" in Spanish) or remo (meaning "oar") is a beverage traditionally drunk in Argentina and Uruguay. It consists of a bar of dark chocolate melted inside a glass of hot milk and stirred with a long spoon (similar to an iced tea spoon) until the chocolate is completely dissolved.
26. Crazy
27. Calm down
28. Advanced tango moves
29. Soap operas
30. An affectionate diminutive of Mari
31. The people who frequent milongas, avid dancers of the tango
32. A Spanish or Latin American pastry turnover filled with a variety of savoury ingredients and baked or fried.
33. Argentinian pizza
34. Uncooked sauce or condiment made with finely chopped parsley, minced garlic, oregano, red chilli flakes, olive oil, and vinegar.
35. Grilled cheese
36. A soft, crumbly cookie sandwich typically with dulce de leche or manjar blanco as a filling.

4. New Year, New You

1. Rice, lentils (black or brown), chickpeas and pasta cooked individually, then tossed together and topped with cumin-scented tomato sauce and crunchy fried onions.
2. Meatballs
3. a stew of cooked lava beans served with olive oil, cumin, and optionally with chopped parsley, garlic, onion, lemon juice, chilli pepper and other vegetable, herb and spice ingredients.

5. Idol

1. A type of spirit or ghost in Korean folklore
2. Virgin Ghost
3. Banana flavoured milk
4. A buckwheat noodle dish
5. Older sister
6. An exclamation expressing displeasure
7. An obsessive fan who stalks or engages in other behaviour constituting an invasion of the privacy of celebrities, specifically Korean idols, drama actors or other public figures.
8. Bitch
9. A Korean alcoholic drink typically made from rice or sweet potatoes

6. The Perfect Wife

1. A Chinese cabbage of a variety with smooth-edged tapering leaves.
2. A Japanese shaved ice dessert flavoured with syrup and a sweetener, often condensed milk

7. Lala Lakshmi

1. A loose collarless shirt
2. Confectioners/ Sweet makers
3. Indian sweets
4. Goddess
5. Mother
6. poori (deep-fried rounds of flour) and aloo (potato) bhaji (a spiced potato dish which may be dry or curried). It is a traditional breakfast dish in North India.
7. Indian bread and chickpea curry
8. A sweet and spicy street-food dish consisting of a mixture of sliced vegetables (especially potatoes and chickpeas) and papri in a yogurt and tamarind sauce
9. An Indian dish of puffed rice, onions, spices, and hot chutney
10. A fast food dish consisting of a thick vegetable curry (bhaji) served with a soft bread roll (pau).
11. A piece of vegetable or meat, coated in seasoned batter and deep-fried.
12. Bitter gourd
13. A type of tie-dye textile decorated by plucking the cloth with the fingernails into many tiny bindings that form a figurative design. The term bandhani is derived from the Sanskrit verbal root bandh ("to bind, to tie").
14. Dial the number!
15. Yes

16. An abusive term

17. A long tunic worn over a pair of baggy trousers.

18. Traditional Indian decoration and patterns made with ground rice, particularly during festivals

19. Dense milk-based sweets

20. Tight trousers worn by people from South Asia, typically with a kameez or kurta.

21. Long scarf

22. A fudge made out of cashews

23. An Indian sweet consisting of a ball of paneer (curd cheese) cooked in syrup

24. A variety of dense, sweet confection or halwa

25. Lentil curry

26. Okra

27. Homespun cotton

28. Grandfather

29. Idiot

30. Indian hand-crafted leather slippers that are locally tanned using vegetable dyes. Kolhapuri Chappals or Kolhapuris as they are commonly referred to are a style of open-toed, T-strap sandal

31. A type of gold thread used decoratively on Indian clothing.

32. Sister

33. Indian flatbread

34. Father

35. A tropical Old World tree, that yields timber resembling mahogany, oil, medicinal products, and insecticide

36. A light bedstead

37. An endearment meaning "my life"

38. An Indian sweet consisting of a ball of deep-fried paneer boiled in a sugar syrup

39. Brother

40. Cauldrons

41. Fat bitter gourd

ACKNOWLEDGMENTS

This is the tricky part! Where do I even begin? So many people have been a part of this journey. This book has been fostered by multiple parents; I just happen to be its birth mother.

Let me begin by thanking my family, and my husband, in particular. Without his 'superman' abilities, I could not be the 'superwoman' everyone thinks I am (I really am not!). My kids who put up with my erratic schedules and sleep patterns because, like an owl or a hamster, I am a nocturnal creature. Thanks *famiglia*! You are the wind beneath my wings.

Now, each story has had people who've helped me with the correct usage of the language and terminology, and without them, I doubt I would have been able to give these tales the slightest whiff of authenticity. Véronique, Celia, Sonia, Mike, Eileen, Prianka - thank you for your input and your feedback. It has proven invaluable.

Next, I must acknowledge my wonderful beta readers - Vibha, Maria, Paul, An, Valerie, Mireille, Hollene and Samantha. Thank you for offering to be my guinea pigs, to read the rough drafts, to point out the errors and discrepancies, and to review the book in a fair and honest fashion. I am deeply grateful that you are a part of my ART team.

My subscribers, you have been just as much a part of this book's journey as anyone else. When I was grappling with the dilemma of whether to include a glossary, the answer to my query was a resounding YES! So, I did. But with the proviso that people could choose to ignore the glossary altogether if they didn't want to cross reference the words. All my wonderful newsletter subscribers' suggestions. Many, many thanks!

My acknowledgements would be incomplete if I did not mention my incredible editor, Charulatha. She is truly a gem, and I hope we have several years of collaborating ahead of us. If you are a writer who is looking for a fantastic editor, drop her a line at: charu.dpp@gmail.com

The cover design is by the amazing MiblArt Team (team@miblart.com), who once again brought my vision to life. We went through multiple iterations before settling on this one, and each time, they were patient and happy to oblige me with different versions. A BIG thank you!

Finally, it is you, my readers, that I burn the midnight oil for. Your response to my stories, your emails that tell me how much you've enjoyed what I've written, your complaints that I haven't released a new book recently... all of this makes it so completely worthwhile!

Thank you and keep writing to me. I love hearing from you. :)

ABOUT THE AUTHOR

With a voracious appetite for reading and an unbridled imagination, Poornima started writing stories at age eight. Newspaper in Education, The Times of India supplement, published several of her winning entries. Over the years, family and career took over and writing took a back seat.

In 2009, when a short story of hers placed in an online competition run by The Guardian newspaper, she once again found her writing voice. Subsequently, she started an online blog where she continued to write articles and stories. Nine years later these stories appeared in two separate books as a part of the India trilogy. Since then, she has published the third book in the trilogy, a novella, another book of short stories and her first novel.

ALSO BY POORNIMA MANCO

Parvathy's Well & other stories

Damage & other stories

Holi Moly! & other stories

The Intimacy of Loss

Twelve - stories from around the world

Parvathy's Well & Other Stories: The India Collection

A Quiet Dissonance